Visits with the
Old Indian Storyteller

ISBN 978-0-9797057-1-7
Printed in the United States by Petals & Pages Press

©2007
as related by Tomi Jill Folk
cover photos and design by Tomi Jill Folk

We express our most sincere appreciation
to Mr. Elmer Leon of the Santa Ana Pueblo,
who sat with two Anglos
surrounded by murals from an ancient kiva,
heard the stories of our journey,
and shared some of his own.

By his respect for our confusion
and search for understanding,
he helped increase our courage
to let these stories now be told.

And to our parents
who read or heard each of the stories that follow,
and were comforted in their journeys,
either beyond life as we know it,
or still walking here, now alone.

Visits with the Old Indian Storyteller

Introduction

My husband talks in his sleep. Not so unusual, one might think, for many people sleep talk. But once in awhile, when the sleep talk begins, the voice is no longer his own. In the cadence of an elderly Native American storyteller, with gestures to match, we have been "visited" by the one known to us only by the title of the Storyteller, or the Old Indian, for "to name me would be to limit me." He comes to us when we need his comfort or challenge the most, with wisdom, advice, and inspiring stories.

At first, I was quite unsettled, for things like this aren't supposed to happen to a fairly conservative Lutheran pastor, which I was at the time it began. My husband had been married before; his first wife swears the sleep talk is an entirely new development. By intuition I sensed something special was happening, and so grabbed a notebook, and tried taking dictation. Where I could not keep up, you will see blanks _____ like this, meaning that I knew I missed something, but couldn't recapture it. More often there would be lengthy pauses between phrases, which I have tried to indicate by the format of leaving spaces between lines.

Eventually, I found that I could sometimes enter into conversation with the Old Indian, and so in the lessons that follow, my words are recorded *in italics*.

Until we arranged a microphone and cassette recorder in such a way as to be able to tape the Old Indian's very soft voice, my husband thought I was creating the stories myself. He had no memories of the conversations. But we did begin to notice that the "visits" would generally happen when he was very stressed, and would be proceeded by a wave of irresistible exhaustion. When he would awaken after an episode, he had no sense of having rested.

When a few others have been allowed to hear the tapes, what surprises them most is the slow, deliberate, almost hypnotic tempo of the storytelling, with extended pauses being quite common. Each "visit" often lasted between a half hour and forty-five minutes, while for someone else to read or tell the stories as written would take far less time.

It was frightening, in the beginning. Eventually, the "visits" grew to mean a lot to us, as the messages were especially helpful while we cared for my husband's mother for the last months of her life. A few times we found the stories confusing, and couldn't quite understand the symbolism he used. But we chose to include those particular stories in the collection, in the hope that they would strike a chord of recognition for someone else. They are arranged in chronological order, with a few notes of explanation as to what events were transpiring in our lives at the time of the "visit."

As writers, we began to wonder if the lessons had been entrusted to us for a purpose. So in April of 1999, I asked the Old Indian. He answered with the following questions:
"What have I done with you? Have I not shared them with you?" *Yes, you have.*
"Then how can you do less, and be in harmony?"
May the stories that follow bring you encouragement, comfort, and hope, as they have done for us.

The Vision Quest

July 15, 1997

Listen! Listen!
      Do you hear the song of the morning wind?

Come over here by the fire--
      we'll greet the sunrise,
      and I will tell you a morning story.

It is about your grandfather, Paulo John,
      who needed to seek his vision.

He would have to cross the Malpais,
      the place where the earth was on fire.
      It's made of the black rock that scientists call basalt.

Paulo John set out to go to Mash-no-ah (Mount Taylor, now.)
He made his trek to the first place, where he made a camp, but there was no water.
      He woke early with a great thirst.

He spoke to the Great Mystery,
and apologized for not understanding how difficult it could be to seek one's vision.

He prayed to be led to water.

As the sun rose, he lifted corn pollen to the morning,
      as we do today, tying ourselves to the ancestors
      and relatives in the future,
      one circle of life, all interconnected.
      But back to Paulo John.

Malpais is difficult, for the lava cuts moccasins,
      and you bleed.

He was gone till almost the heat of day,
      till he heard the moan and cry and saw the buzzards circle to the north.

He approached quietly,
      as is the way when we don't know what we will find.
      Fear holds us back; curiosity drives our feet forward.

Some scrub, salt bush; few trees.

In the shade, he heard the moan, the cry of death,
      and the buzzards came closer.
      He had to throw stones to keep them away.

He saw the Belagaana (white man) who had fallen--
      his leg was bent under him.
      There was much blood on the ground.

Paulo John did not smell death--
      the buzzards were only waiting.
He was in a quandary.
If he were to help this man, he'd have to forgo his quest.
But he could see the canteen beside the cowboy.

He stood, and called "Hola," the call of friendship.
The Belagaana turned his head,
      and at the sight of Paulo John,
      he tried to reach for his carbine,
          which was too far away.

He said, "Please don't hurt me--I am dying."

Paulo John kneeled beside him,
      helped straighten his leg,
          gathered splints from the salt bush,
          then gave the cowboy a drink from the canteen,
              and had one himself.

They didn't speak the same language.
But the cowboy knew he couldn't leave without Paulo John.
Paulo John knew he could take the water, but how could he leave him?

He stayed, built a fire, cleansed the wound,
      both suspicious of each other,
          knew they needed each other.

Paulo John fashioned a crutch, slept, and the next morning continued the journey.

It took four more days to cross the Malpais.

Paulo John knew others would think he'd failed
      and gone to meet the Great Mystery,
      but he had to stop to treat the wound.

As they cleared the lava flow,
      where they took the path to the south,
      the food was gone. It was not the season of berries.

They came to a cabin where the cowboy lived,
      where Paulo John was welcomed, too.

He explained his quest for a vision,
      that he had to climb Mash-no-ah.
Cowboy and his family gave Paulo John food:
      jerky, dried apples, bread, and a canteen of water.

Paulo John was provisioned,
      and made great speed on his climb.
In two days, he got to the top,
      set the fires, gave his prayers.

As he slept, he had his vision.

There was a great field, with flowers of all colors.
The flowers lived in great harmony.
      Each was visited by a hummingbird,
      who brought great knowledge from the Great Mystery.

He walked over to the flowers,
      and saw that they were the faces of people--
      he was to extend understanding to all people,
         just as he had with the cowboy.

On the return, he stopped at the cabin,
      and was pleased to see the wound had healed.

He gave them his corn pollen,
      and showed them to scatter a pinch
         to the morning sun to bring blessings.

He invited them to visit him at Acoma.

This is not the end, my children.

You are a part of this chapter,
          and your children are the next chapter
                    in this book that is always being written,
                              the great book of friendship.

The apple slices are warm; eat them,
          and go gather the squash blossoms,
                    and have a good day.

It is good to have children, to hear the stories.
It is good to have elders, to tell the stories
Without the stories, they don't know where they belong,
          and it is important for all of us to know where we belong.

There always have been storytellers,
          and will be,
                    as long as there is someone to listen.

Now, if you'll excuse me, I have some sheep to tend.

          (What a mystery this first story was! My husband had attended college in New Mexico, but I had not spent any time there, and had never heard of the places described. Hank told me about the locations after reading the story the next morning. It was not a familiar tale to him, although we both appreciated the message. And by mentioning that Paulo John was from the Pueblo at Acoma, for a long time we thought that the Storyteller was also from Acoma. It would be several years before we learned that he is connected with many other places.)

The Rosary
July 25, 1997

I remember cool evenings, working outside in the yard.

I remember one particular evening,
      so cold that we wore blankets
      as we moved about our tasks.

I was five on that cold evening,
      and one of the old men had built a bonfire.

And he invited the children
      to come near to the fire he had built.

I was one of those children, and this is the story he told us:

"Come close and warm your hands,
      Come closer, and warm your hearts."

As we sat, he told us to watch the flames,
      that in the flames
      were the messages of the Great Mystery.

We could see much by watching the ever-changing flames,
      the logs, and the sparkles.

He taught us of the rhythms of the flames.
They danced to the slow and steady beat of his drum.
He told us to relax as we watched the light,
      and he taught us to draw the light into us,
          and become one with it.

Then he set aside his drum.

Instead, he played the flute.
      We became very relaxed,
      and saw ourselves dancing within the flames.

He opened the medicine bag,
     and took out a string of beads.
     We'd seen these beads before--
         Some Belagaana wore them around their necks,
         others carried them in their pockets.

He told us it was no problem to see clearly.
     He held up the beads to the light.

He explained that the flames viewed from me on his left
     were different than those seen by Paulo on his right,
         but it was all the same fire.

He held up the beads for all of us to see--
     ____ Jesu Christo used these beads to remember their prayers.
         A necklace of roses, "por la rosa esta la flor del Jesu Christo."

These beads we could see were shiny black seeds;
     spaced between groups of these seeds were other seeds of turquoise.

He explained to us that they had three prayers they had to remember,
     and this reminded them of Hail Mary,
     Maria la Madre del Jesu Christo.

He told us the Hispanios had a primitive religion;
     they had an imperfect understanding of the Great Mystery,
     and they hailed the Great Mystery as a man,
     and hailed the mother of the man, Maria.

They gave one of their prayers to Maria, their woman god, this one they called "Hail Mary."
     Because they were primitive, they considered themselves children,
         ____ reminded them of the Our Father,
     because they viewed the Great Mystery as the Father in the sky.

Foolish, for we know that the Great Mystery is everywhere.
     We worship in food, dance, on mountains and in valleys.

He said the Great Mystery told us to be kind to these people who didn't have great
understanding.

The last prayer, the Glory Dei which was kind of a collective prayer
     since they weren't sure what the Great Mystery was.

They pray to the Father, Son, Holy Spirit, whatever the Great Mystery was.

He explained that we should always try to understand how others see the Great Mystery.
Like sitting around the great fire, each sees a different flame,
      but it is all the same fire.

He told us of the great good done by the people with the ro-sa-ree.
      He passed it around.
      The beads were the seeds of a flower in the family of the iris, called Job's tears.
      He said that was an appropriate seed to use,
      because like the character, he explained that flowers had a (his voice drifted off.)

Job was a character in the Old Book they followed.
      The tears were from a member of the iris family--some call it a grass--
      in a tribe that lived far away in time and place, a tribe called the Egyptians,
      who valued the iris as the bringer of sight.

He said this rosaree is beautiful in the way each seed is precisely drilled,
      and each turquoise is precisely smoothed and carved.
      He told us to examine it closely--we did.

He told us that it was made by a blind lady.

While her sight had been taken by the years, her vision became sharper.
      So she made the rosarees for the illumination of all her friends,
      a gift of light for everyone.

I as a child did not think this much of a story.

I listened politely, as I warmed my hands and watched the flames.

Now I understand what grandfather was saying.
      When I have my eyes closed, I can still see the flames,
      the mountains beyond in the distance,
      the frogs in the pond.

When I close my eyes, I do not see, but I envision.

What he tried to tell us is that while we all see the Great Mystery differently,
      we all have the vision to do good things that will please the Great Mystery.

I understand now, that Grandfather was a wise man.

(Hank then rolled over and said in a different voice:
   "The flowers of Job's tears grow on a stalk about 2 feet high.
   The flowers are small blue or lavender,
   The seeds are shiny black, and they hang each on a string of its own,
        a seed stalk has 20 or 30 seeds hanging from it.")

(Hank is a garden writer and horticultural therapist. Upon reading this story again in 1999, he found it hard to understand why the plant was referred to as an iris, rather than as a member of the grass family, which the Old Indian alluded to. This is one of the clues that the Old Indian is not just a part of Hank's mind, but a different entity entirely. In several other stories, vocabulary words that are totally unfamiliar to Hank are used. We have been unable to find some of the terms used in any dictionary, either. All are part of the mystery of the stories.

For me as a pastor, the heart of this story is that the Great Mystery is more incredible and undefinable than the way any of us perceive or describe God. My faith tradition is quite dogmatic and systematic in its theological interpretations; what a delight for me to hear God described as bigger and better than all of that.)

Cooperation
August 6, 1997

Shhhhhhh.
Listen to the voice of the fire.

Do you see the lesson in the glare?

There is warmth there, and light,
      but look, if I pull one of these branches out, the flame fades.

The fire is more than the total of the flames of each stick.

Our Pueblo is like that. (His arm swept across bed.)

If each of us is alone, we would be like the tiny fire, and---

But when each stick is combined together, we light the whole street.
      Everyone's hands are warmed.

When we all gather together in the Pueblo, it is like all the branches together burning.
      Each stick makes a contribution to the fire.
      Each flame is the work of that stick.

Each of us carries a flame inside us, and it is our job, our duty, to find someone to carry it on.

Remember this afternoon, when the women gathered at the matates to grind the corn--
      we had the young women grind first, to break the kernels, then the cracked corn....
      Then lastly, the finatate takes infinitely more....

If each of us has a job, if each makes a contribution to the Pueblo, it will survive and thrive.

As the women are grinding the corn, the old ones play the flute or bang the drum.
This is done, to make the work easier.......

14

The Cracked Pot
August 11, 1997

Come on over and sit down.
You've had a difficult day today. I know.
I want to tell you a little story.

Not all stories are of the long ago time.
Some stories are of the nearly yesterdays.
Some stories are of tomorrows.

You are small, and have only a few years to look back on,
  and many to look forward to.
When you are young, it is the years ahead that are your burden;
  but when you are old,
  it is the years past that are the heavy weight on your shoulders.

There are many, many young people who, like you, have the joy of much to learn,
  the thrill of much to see.

I want to tell you about a little Anglo boy,
  because while we are all different,
  we are like the leaves of the sassafras or mulberry;
   different leaves, on the same tree.

In the far away land we call the orient, the mulberry is a sacred tree.
  To us, all trees are sacred; As yet, their understanding is incomplete.
  However, the Great Mystery works inside all of us,
   the Anglos with the fast tongue,
   or Chicanos who sing the beautiful songs,
   or one of us, who seeks the great harmonies.

The Great Mystery doesn't care what language we speak;
  the Great Mystery knows them all.

That is the great knowledge of the Great Mystery;
  our winding path is to learn to understand each other.

You tend sheep--it is your place in our pueblo.
Not far from here, on a single pueblo called a ranch,
  there was a young boy, small for his years.

Words he heard most often were "no" and "don't" and "you can't do that,"
       for this is the way of the Anglos,
         spending time telling their children what they *can't* do,
         rather than showing them the wonderful and joyful things they *can* do.

This little boy got so tired of being told "no" and "don't" and "you can't do that"
       that he would walk by the big rocks up on the canyon wall,
         and watch the calves.

Each calf was very important; each calf was needed to build their herd.

The Anglos didn't understand the buffalo, and killed them
       and got cattle that need much care.
The buffalo needed no care. They followed the sun, and gave us many gifts.
       Perhaps one day, the Anglo will understand.

This day had been particularly hard for the boy--
       he was small, and didn't know he wasn't strong.
       When the body lacks the strength, and mind lacks the knowledge, it is sad.

He wandered off with a loaf of bread, leather pouch, and his mother's jelly.

He walked up into the canyon, looking down, a smart thing to do,
       but Anglos look at the horizon, and trample their greatest gifts at their feet.

He was looking down, because he had found several pieces of shiny stone.
       He saw a roadrunner chase a snake--
       He heard jays in the background--
       He saw a horned toad chase a beetle and catch it--
       He watched a spider build a web.

He was watching in particular a little deer mouse--
       you know, the one with big white feet--
       scurry over the pot our grandfathers of many years ago had made.

The lip was broken, and it was partly buried,
       and it was filled with sand and dirt,
       and a tough little sprig of gramma grass grew from it.

He picked it up, and dumped it out.
       It held the nest of a pack rat, and the gems it had left behind.
       Some obsidian, and dry flowers;

Anglos don't take time to teach their children the name of the plants,
    so to him they were only flowers;
    pretty, one time beautiful;
    a little coin, a little flake of pyrite;
    treasures to a pack rat, a curiosity to the boy.

He was intrigued by the markings. It was almost a pitcher, but the lip was broken.

He carried it, and came to a seep.
    He rinsed it, then drank. It was good.
    He didn't know who made it, but he felt the magic of it bridging years.
He had in his mind an image of times past,
    and saw the people using the pot and others.

He was contemplating this, and heard jays squawking, and he heard a calf bleat.
    He knew that calves are important; this one sounded injured.
    He stood and listened hard to hear a direction, but there was only silence.

Then, in his own silence, he heard it again.
    It sounded so sad and weak, an animal without hope.
He went in the direction he thought he heard it, still carrying the pitcher of water.

He clamored on the rocks, looked around cactus, and under the juniper.
    It was very close.
    He stumbled and saw where some rocks had fallen down the talus---
    With only the head and shoulders showing was the calf, crying for help.
    It looked very weak.

Carefully, he crawled down the rocks. He petted to comfort it, gave it water,
    talked to it, gave it the bread and water.

He tried to move the stones, but the rocks were too heavy for him.
    He gave the calf the last of the water, and started back to his cabin.

When he got to his home, he brought his father back.
    Together they could move the big rocks to free the calf.

His father picked it up and carried it back.
    The boy picked up the pitcher and carried it back.

The father bragged to everyone who came to their place,
    of how his son saved the calf.

The boy kept the pitcher in his room, and looked at it each morning,
and he knew that even if the day was full of "no's" and "don't" and "you can'ts,"
      there was much that he *could* do.
          He had saved a life, a good thing for a young boy to do.

I tell you this, because often you also dwell on your limits--the can'ts--
and you need to know that isn't just the burden of the young, but also elders.

But the Great Mystery, in great wisdom, gives us each a pot.
      Our job is to recognize it, fill it, and use it in all the ways that we can.

Recognize the gifts the Great Mystery has given you,
      and discover the ways they can be used to do good.

Now go, dael, [little one] and tend your sheep.

I asked him, "And who are you, Grandfather?
With a smile, he answered, "The Storyteller."

"By what name are you called?

I am only known as the Old Indian, for to name me would be to limit me.

      Someday, you will understand my mystery.

      Some hear my words and fear me, and call me evil names.
      Others use my knowledge.
      Some are wise enough to glory and enjoy each of my gifts.

      Very few understand that I am more than now,
            I am more than before,
         and I am more than what will be.

I give great gifts, and they are wasted,
      but I am patient,

      and I understand that so much of what we do is learning about ourselves,
         and what is within us--that is the most fearful,
        for we don't want to know what we are.

This is foolish, for all are part of the Great Mystery;
      that makes each one of us so special.

Tend your sheep, and dwell on the "I can do this, I can know that."
These carry the burdens for you.

(He was right; it had been a difficult day for me. Hank's mother, who lived with us, was fast fading in strength from congestive heart failure, and it was becoming increasingly difficult for me to properly care for her. She had agreed that it was time for us to ask for help from our local hospice, which is a traumatic decision for many families. I felt like a failure. And then, the Old Indian told this story.

The very next day, Hank was sorting donations that had just arrived at the thrift store where he volunteered. Buried in the pile was a pitcher, hand made of pottery, broken at the lip. It rests on the shelf above my computer, for this particular story continues to influence my life.

As a pastor, I had served congregations in Minnesota and South Dakota. Three times within seven years, floods caused two of my locations to be declared national disaster areas. In addition, we had also faced two tornadoes that damaged farm buildings and crops. Clergy and local police played a primary role in helping people find the assistance they needed at the immediate time, and perhaps more importantly, were there to provide emotional support long after the crises passed. Like many others, I was exhausted. A virus we called "the crud" claimed me and many others, and wouldn't allow me to return to strength for weeks. A medication given to treat the crud nearly killed me.

That was in October of 1993; I went on temporary disability, expecting recovery to take weeks, or possibly several months. In May of 1994 it was obvious that the process would take even longer, so I resigned from my parish, and moved to Florida to be near my family. Two years later, it was here that I met the man who would soon become my husband. And somehow, through our union, these stories emerged.

Now I look at the damaged pot on the shelf, and hear the "no, don't, and you can't do that" messages, and I wonder exactly what I still can do, and what it is I know, and what sheep God still has for me to tend. And I wonder at how the Old Indian found and chose us, and who he really is.)

"*For we have this treasure in clay jars,* so that it may be made clear that this extraordinary power belongs to God and does not come from us." 2 Corinthians 4:5-7 New Revised Standard Version of the Bible.

The Story of the Blanket

August 24, 1997

It is cold tonight.
Here, take this blanket.
There is warmth in the blanket.
Come, sit over here and talk, and I will tell you the story of the blanket.

This is a story of long, long ago, when ours were the only people here.

It is the story of Napalo--
Napalo, a young girl in a family of weavers.

This was in the old days before we had wool,
    we wove our blankets of cotton and yucca fiber.
    We made the dyes in the old way--we did not buy them at K-mart.

Napalo's parents were famous for their weaving,
    and made blankets for all special ceremonies.

Napalo did not have the gift of working the warp and the woof,
    and her parents would ridicule her.

She would sit under the cottonwood trees with children younger than she was,
    and tell good stories,
        about how coyote put the stars in the sky,
        about the fire people in the mountains,
        and how the people came from underground into the world of light.

She told the stories very well, but her parents criticized her.

Gradually, the whole village would gather to hear her stories.
    She would sit by the fire, and children gathered,
    and parents, too, in the front row,
    for they hadn't heard;
    or heard and forgot,
    or just enjoyed hearing them again, for Napalo was a great storyteller.

Napalo collected the stories, but her family was angry,
    and thought that she wasted her time.

20

So, she left, and she walked as far as her feet would take her,
      and then sat on a rock.

Napalo saw the spider spinning a beautiful web.
      As you know, the spider taught us how to weave.
            She asked, "Grandmother Spider, will you teach me to weave?"

The spider laughed and said, "Foolish child, you already have the gift of weaving."

"No, I can't. The looms don't work in my hands. The shuttle doesn't flow.
      I make mistakes, and ruin blankets." Napalo replied.

The spider laughed again. "No, that is not the work that you do.
      You have the gift of weaving words into a beautiful blanket,
            and words bring warmth and comfort, as well as the fabric."

Napalo was pleased with this news.

She was very glad, and fell asleep.

In the land of the dream people where she was a guest,
      she was led to a place with a hillside near a stream, where blue water flowed.

She saw a lonely Indian man, small in stature, old, very old.
      Slowly, he would load the cuddles(?) into his shuttle,
      and push it through the warp to make beautiful designs.
      The blanket was almost finished.

Napalo watched each thread take longer and longer to go through the warp.
      The colors were beautiful; the pattern, too.
      Some sections were pale, some gray, some bright designs.

Napalo watched and watched and watched,
      as this Indian put the last thread through, and freed the shuttle of its thread.

The Indian took the blanket from the loom.
      It had been a long day, and was evening.
      It was cold; he built a small fire to warm his hands.
      He trimmed and tied the fringes of the blanket.

      He lay down and covered himself; then, he was gone.

"Do you understand the meaning of the story?" Spider asked.

Napalo bowed her head, embarrassed by her ignorance.

"It is simply this," The spider told Napalo. "Look on the banks of the river."

There were children, young people, and adults, all busy weaving blankets.

"Why are they all weaving beautiful blankets?" Napalo asked.

Some were only begun. Others were complete enough to show a pattern.
Some were dull and drab; some were confusing.

The spider said, "Do you not see what is happening here?"

"No," Napalo replied.

"These are all the people in the world, weaving their soul blankets.
Have you not heard of the soul blankets?"

Napalo shook her head, ashamed of her ignorance.

The spider said, "We all begin to weave a blanket at birth, the blanket for our soul.
Each action is a thread--watch and you can follow the patterns of our life.

When our work is done, the soul blanket is complete.
We wrap ourselves in it when we go to the great sleep,
where we visit the Great Mystery."

Napalo asked, "There is a child, who has almost completed his blanket?"

Spider responded, "Yes, he is almost done, and will go on his soul journey soon.
Do not think that one's work is only done when old and feeble.
For many, their work is done when they are young and active;
for some, work is done when they fall in battle.

Others' work is done when they lay down with sickness,
and don't wake up.

It is not our doing to pick the time when the blanket is done.
All we can do is live lives so our soul can make beautiful patterns and bright colors."

Napalo returned from the dreamland people, and told these stories,
and everyone was happy.

Now, you can tell Napalo's stories, too,
as the tradition of the people of words is as strong as that of the weaving people.

Now go, and weave your blanket of words.

(If the last story was for me, this one was for Hank. He came from a family of expert carpenters, gifted at using their hands to create wonders with wood, who have never quite understood his thirst for education and drive to write.

The story was for all of us, actually, for we were keeping vigil at his mother's side, asking hard questions about why such a wonderful person would soon leave us. We found comfort in knowing that she had woven a fine blanket throughout her eighty-four years of life. In her memory the following year Hank wrote *The Family Caregiver's Journal, A Guide to Facing the Terminal Illness of a Loved One*. We included the story of The Blanket, in the hope that it would comfort others as they wrestle with the same concerns regarding whether a loved one was dying "too soon," or exactly when his or her blanket is finished.)

The Music of Life

August 27, 1997

(Started with a smile.)

So, you like the sound of the drums, do you?
Did you know that music makes the corn crop grow?

Here, this is the seed pot that we store the seeds of the corn, the seeds of the beans,
     the seeds of the chilies, the seeds of the squash in, as well as the lettuce seeds.
The tiny little hole in the top of the pot--back in the ancient days,
     a stick was put in the hole, and sealed it, and kept out the insects and mice.

Each family had its special seed pots. Different clans grew different kinds of corn.
That is why even today we have people from the red corn clan,
     the blue corn clan, and the yellow corn clan.
     And we have the different squash and different beans.
          These were family traditions.

You are asking me what is the connection
     between the seeds and the beat of the drum.

Come a little closer. Listen to the beat of the drum.
Here, put your head on my chest,
     and listen to the beat of the drum within each of us.

Do you not hear the music of life in the heart drum?
It is the music of life in the heart drum.

In the ancient days, when people planted corn with a stick and a drum,
     as the seed was planted, the drum was played.

Life of the corn started in the sound of the drum.
     This is an important lesson.

We have had in our village/pueblo for centuries drums and flutes,
     and our children learn to play the music and sing the songs.

In the circle of time in one of the agos,
     there came the people from Spain, across the ocean we now call the Atlantic.
These people came to our villages and shared some gifts with us,
     they shared the gift of sheep, the gift of apples, and the gift of peaches.

24

There were many others.

In some ways, these people were very selfish, and they taught us what tax meant.
    We grew our corn, and gave it to them, to defend us from enemies.
    Ancestors thought this strange, had done it for centuries without them.

They brought their religion; the Great Mystery they called God.

They brought their way of thinking and seeing.
Their God had a son, Jesu Christo,
    and their God had priests,
    who did not wear great costumes of shells or bells on their ankles.

Their priests were very drab and dressed like a mouse in a brown cloak.
    Their priests called themselves "Franciscans"
    and they brought the songs that they sing to their gods.
    The songs were called chants. We'd never heard anything quite like this.

I was then reminded that with the Franciscan priest and their chants,
    there were also many people whose skins were very dark.
    In those days, they were called Moors. They were Spanish, too.

The Moors brought their special kind of music.
The Moors brought their music from Africa,
    and where our ancestor's Pueblo had known our drum and flute,
    now they had big drums
    and African music which was very lively, very enthusiastic.

The corn grows when we sing to it,
    because we sing the song of life,
    and beat the drum to our inner drive of life.
As the corn grows, the weather is hot and dry, and we sing and dance in a circle around the fire.
While we dance, we pray that the Great Mystery will send water,
and again a second time we pray, that the Great Mystery won't send too much.

It was very kind for the Hispanios and Africans to give their music and add their voices.
The music in the Pueblo is not ours alone.
    It is shared, and what a glory it is, to be shared.

It is this lesson,
    that music is something to be shared,
        which is important to you.

There is so much to learn of our musical heritage.

Music is harmony; the essence of life is harmony.

It is very important to the spirit inside you to sing your song, play your drums, put your flute to your lips; and those of you who have taken up the guitar, do well.

Do not be afraid to lend your Father's way to your children.
(What does that mean? To teach the old songs?)
Yes, of course, you should know that, for that is the meaning of tradition.

We can't live in the past. We can't live in the future.
We can sing and dance in the present.
      Come, and play the drum.

Harmony is the blend of the past and future, where we stand in the present.

When we sing of life, and dance to our inner drum,
      we are at harmony with all life,
      and are at peace with ourself.

Does that conclude the lesson?
Are you going to dance?
Oh, probably.
Then the lesson is complete.

(As Mum declined, I so dearly wanted to be of assistance, but didn't have the physical strength necessary. So she asked me to sing to her. I could play guitar and sing any songs, as long as the first was "In the Garden," and the second song was "How Great Thou Art." It became part of the tradition for any visitor to be invited to join in the songs.

One of the holy moments of that last month came as a hospice nurse prepared to leave. We sang together; then she asked if we would mind if she sang a special spiritual as a goodbye prayer. Her voice filled the small room, overflowing to bless our entire house. With Mum's devotion to us, and so many gracious acts from family and guests, the very walls of her room became saturated with love. After she died, I chose to make her bedroom into my study.)

The Choice
September 1, 1997

(Not everyone supported our decision to keep Mum at home. This story was told the night before certain guests arrived, who thought she should be in a nursing home, instead.)

This is a decision we all must make.
It is a decision, to prepare yourself for tomorrow.

Sit down. I've got a little story for you.
It takes place at a comfortable, relaxed place. Here, have an apple.

It takes place long, long from now. Not all stories are long, long ago.
      This is long, long yet to come.

There was a small child, and he was playing in a dry arroyo,
      and the storms came,
      and when the storm water came, he was washed away.

And his mother was very upset.
She searched and searched, until she found him gasping for life.
She rescued him, and took him home.

The winter came. Snow fell, and water became ice.

And the dark shaman came to the village,
      and he sat in the plaza carving, polishing, chipping away on a piece of ice.
      He carved a face in the ice.
      Beside the face was a hand. At the tip of each finger was a flower.

The dark shaman took the carving to the mother of the little boy,
      in order to gain her favors.
He told her that if she put it in the window, and kept the house cold,
      the sun would glow through it.
      Each flower was a different color,
      and a rainbow would splash the wall and paint it with its glow.

She was taken with it.
He said the face was meant to be hers, but it was only half as beautiful.
      She like beauty, especially her own.

He reminded her to keep it cold, or the sculpture would melt.

She took the logs from the fire. Her child cried, "I am cold!"
She knew that she must keep the home cold, or the beautiful ice face would melt,
        so she put another blanket on the child.

He cried that he would die if she didn't make it warm.

She had to decide,
        for she couldn't have both the beautiful face, or the love of her child.

What do you think she decided?

What would you decide, if you were her?
        Think on this, for the answer is in your heart.

We all face this decision---
        it is the decision to live a cold life, and have possessions,
        or to live a warm life, and have love.

This is your decision, too, so think on it.

I see you are warming your hands by the fire---that is good.
        By what fire do you warm your heart?

        What's this you say?
        You don't warm your heart; your friends do.

That is a wise answer. The warmth of love keeps your heart warmed.

More important--
        it is you who can make other people's hearts warm.
        Think on this, for it is an important lesson.

Now, tell me, which did she choose?
        The face, or her child?
                Which would you choose?

The Shapes of Life

early September, 1997

You cannot live your life like a straight line.
>If you do, you'll never get there.

If you are at the cottonwood, and you go west,
>when you reach the corner, then where you were is east,
>and you haven't gotten west yet.

If you go on, then the corner that was west is now east. So it goes.

So if you live your life as a straight line, take it from here to there,
it never happens,
>and you live your life as a failure.

Some live their life as a triangle.
They start living very hard, and gradually move slower and slower until they come to the point of
the triangle, and they have no idea of where else to go.
>That life is a failure as well.

But some are wise, and live life as a circle,
>because look at the beauty of a circle. It has no beginning or end.

These are the wise ones, as a circle goes on and on and on forever.
These live entire lives in the circle of their spirits.
These are the wise ones.

Their life reflects the earth itself, which is a circle,
>and heaven above, which is a circle.

Think on it.

We call these things the shapes of life: the straight line, the triangle, and the circle.

(This was perhaps the most confusing lesson to us, in part because we were becoming so
exhausted as caregivers. Intuitively, it makes some sense; yet the imagery is beyond our immediate
understanding. Someone from another culture who reads it may find great insight. We hope to grasp
its meaning someday.)

The Hummingbird

September 28, 1997

(Unlike the other lessons, which were delivered during sleeptalk, this one came to Hank very early one morning as he was working on the computer. It was only two days after his mother had left us on her journey to the Great Mystery. We had found peace with the idea that her life was complete, and it was time for her to go to God. But her intense pain as the end neared, even with morphine being used, caused us great distress. Like birth, the transition to the new reality does not always come easily.

The format of this story is different, in that it was recorded by Hank, who writes in paragraphs, rather than by me, Tomi, who hears the phrases of a poet. But like with the sleep talk, when the story was completed, Hank had no memory of what had been said. We read it together when I awoke, and both agreed that our friend, the Old Indian, had to have sent it.)

The old Indian worked with the fire. First he twisted the grass into a ring. In the middle of this, he placed the dried moss and threads of yucca fiber. He carefully laid out the handful of bark and the twigs. The little girl handed him the pot that had the holes in it, the firepot that had the smoke climbing from the top.

He reached in with his fingers and removed the glowing coals. "Fire is a living thing. It finds its birth in our breath." He placed the coals on the moss and blew gently. Nola added her breath, and the yucca fibers began to glow; smoke began its journey skyward.

"It is the way with our people that everyone has a purpose," the old one spoke as he fed twigs to the infant blaze. Nola, desiring to have purpose herself, carefully placed several shreds of bark on the fire. She enjoyed her time with Grandfather. He was too old to work the fields. He didn't even have the breath to play the bird flute like he did when she was a baby. It took great pain for him to descend into the kiva when the clan needed his counsel, but he did his work well. He was the *keeper of the fire*. True, some of the younger men, careless in their thoughts would use the Bic instead of the traditional flint, but even they respected Grandfather for both his wisdom and his knowledge. He had taught them that wisdom was universal to all and was learned from within. Knowledge was harvested from outside, each person sowing and harvesting his or her own fields.

They sat quietly and enjoyed the gifts of the small fire. Warmth for the body, light that played with the shadows on the plaza and the sides of the buildings for the eyes, comforting fragrance from the smoke for the nose, and warm food for the tongue, these were all gifts the fire gave to its friends. But, most important was the comfort the flames gave to the soul, and that was what Nola needed most this evening.

30

"Grandfather, I know Grandmother is very old, and it is the Great Mystery's way that the spirit of each of us is taken to receive the gifts in the far place. These things I know in my heart because Grandmother taught us the stories."

"Your grandmother showed you what was already in your heart. It is through the stories that we all see the wisdom we already have. Grandmother's stories are like these flames casting light for your spirit. The difference is that the light from the stories never burns out, but stays to warm your heart forever." There was the pain of age in his arm as he added more juniper branches to the fire.

"I know here," she touched her head, "that Grandmother was filled with love and gave kindness to all. I know here," she placed her hand on her heart, "that she doesn't deserve the pain she has now."

"You know that your Grandmother has told you her last story. What you don't know is what the Great Mystery plans for her. While she has been so ill, have you not learned important lessons about yourself?"

"What do you mean, Grandfather?"
"Did you not learn compassion when you dried her tears?
  Did you not learn humility when you bathed her and washed her feet?
  Did you not learn that you possessed greater strength, greater kindness,
      greater love than you knew you had?
  Did you not learn something of life by preparing for her death?
  Has she not continued to teach your heart lessons,
      while hers stumbles under its heavy load of many years?"

Nola pondered her Grandfather's questions in silence for many minutes. It is not the way of the Belagaana to think in silence, but for us sometimes the tongue must be still and the drum silent before we can hear the voices that are within us.

The doctors at the hospital in Grants had told them that Grandmother's heart had attacked her. Grandfather had scoffed at such an idea. He knew the life drum that beat within his woman was filled with love. He knew that it was tired. He knew that all hearts beat the song of life until the Great Mystery begins preparations for the journey of great discoveries.

He tried to comfort Nola by explaining the journey, but his skills were not those of a storyteller. He was a wise farmer; he thought deeply and gave good counsel in the kiva, but he was not good at the art of the storyteller. He could skillfully build the fires, play drum and flute, even now he could sing the chants and even dance some of the dances, but his tongue tripped on the words when he tried to tell the stories. He could, in the ancient way knap flint, weave fine baskets of grass and yucca fiber, and even make pottery that the tourists sought, but he could not make the stories.

31

He broke her silence, "Nola, do you know the story of how the people came by the seeds that sustain us here?"

"Oh, yes, Grandfather! Didn't Grandmother tell you about the turkey who carried the seeds under her wings from the great flooding of the underground to the fourth world of light where we are now?" Her voice possessed enthusiasm as she told him the story of the first seeds.

"Do you know where the stars came from?" Grandfather asked with a look of grave seriousness in his eyes, but with a hint of a smile across his lips.

"Everyone knows about how Coyote scattered the stars across the heavens." But she told the story to him with a joy in her heart.

Grandfather's smile was so broad now that it couldn't be hidden. Without prompting, she spoke the stories of the fox, first man and first woman, the water boy, the corn mother, the salt mother, stories of the deer's generosity, the rabbit's cowardice, the raven's wisdom. She talked long into the night with her grandfather. With each story she found her joy doubled, until finally she told him of the hummingbird, the messenger who carries our words to the Great Mystery.

He added more branches to the fire and took from his pouch the bone flute that had been his grandfather's. He played softly for several minutes. Slowly he plied his fingers so that she could watch. Then he handed it to her. "It is good for a storyteller to play the flute while those who have listened have time to think on what you have said."

She took the flute and held it in her hands for several minutes, trying to understand what it was Grandfather had said. Then she put it to her lips.

"It is the wisdom within, the knowledge of what we are," Grandfather said with a smile, "that ties us to the generations past and the children to come. We do not have to make these discoveries ourselves. We don't make the life journey in solitude. The Great Mystery would not do that to his children."

"Grandfather, I understand that Grandmother is dying. I know that is the way we begin the great journey. I am pleased that you think me worthy to continue the tradition of Grandmother. This is an honor I will carry with pride and humility."

"You are still troubled, Child. If you will share with me the heavy load that is on your heart it will become bearable."

"WHY! Grandfather, why does she have to have the pain? I go in to take her the broth and she cries in pain. I bathe her and she is in pain. Even when I sing to her she has pain. Why does the Great Mystery do this to her?"

"Some people do not respect pain. They delight in watching others suffer, even if it is pretend in the Belagaana movies or their coyote cartoons. We do not know the Great Mystery's ways, but it is spoken that some of us are chosen for a special place after we make the journey. Others, perhaps become the hummingbirds that carry our prayers to the Great Mystery itself, and bring back the answers. Other spirits, once freed from their earth body become our *spirit guides.*"

"Grandmother has spoken many times of these creatures that watch over us, keep us from picking the wrong mushroom, guiding our steps among the rocks where the rattlesnake lives, guiding us to the herb that is needed to heal someone's suffering. But I still don't understand. Does everyone have a spirit guide?"

"Yes. Sometimes we foolishly ignore our guardian, but we all have one."

"How does one become a spirit guide? How is one chosen?"

"The Great Mystery, it is said, seeks the kindest hearts, the people on earth most filled with love, and those most able to give it. These are the ones that are trained to become spirit guides. Don't you think that Grandmother is such a person?"

"Yes, but I still don't understand why she has to have the pain."
"Do you know story of Jesu Christo?"

She nodded and then shuddered at the thought of a people so cruel they could nail someone to a tree and watch him die.

"It has been said that to those to whom great gifts are given, much is expected." Grandfather explained. "Your Grandmother will receive great gifts, and the greatest of these is that she will be able to continue to shower love on you. What you see as pain, is as much preparation for you as it is for her. Pain is felt by the body, questioned by the mind, understood by the soul. If we did not feel the pain of your grandmother, would we be worthy of the Great Mystery's gifts to us? If her body did not feel its pain, would her soul be able to understand her new gift?"

"Grandfather," Nola was trying to grasp all of this, to find some comfort in his words. "If Grandmother becomes a spirit guide, will she be mine?"

"I have no doubt."

"What shape will she take? She told me once that her spirit guide was the fox, and," at this point she almost giggled, "that yours was the coyote, because you have done so many foolish things."

33

The old Indian laughed and his hands thumped on the drum as emphasis. After the laughter passed for both of them, he stared into the flames, trying to catch the vision that would answer her question. While he studied smoke and flame, she practiced the tones of the flute.

His old eyes saw through clouds, but the image that appeared in the rising smoke was clear.

"She will come to you as a hummingbird, for she is doubly blessed."

The Great Mystery
November 9, 1997

(With Mum's death behind us, we became more curious about the one who had helped us face it. I had questions ready the next time he returned. Only in rereading this months later did I recognize that he had given answers to my questions, even before I tried to engage him in conversation. My mind was so busy trying to remember what I wanted to ask, that I didn't hear or understand what he was already revealing. Or perhaps I did not connect that what he said of the Great Mystery, was also true of our relationship.)

It is a cold evening.
You are welcome to join me at my fire,
  and find comfort, and warm your hands.

And I am pleased that you come with a bundle of sticks,
  so that you can keep the flames going.
  This is a courtesy, and it is good.

When you feed your sticks into my fire,
  we both feel the warmth, and both are comforted,
  and both can relax in the light.
  There is a lesson of cooperation here.

The smoke smells so good,
  and the apples by the edge of the fire
  are warm and juicy--help yourself.

You seem to be troubled.
  Does not the warmth of the flames
  and the comfort of their light ease your burden?

(Chuckling) You are funny.

You say that you are troubled
  because you do not understand the Great Mystery.

Look at it logically- - -
  if you understood it, it would not be a mystery.
You are like the Anglos who read their books called a mystery novel;
  when they finish it and know how it ends,
  they discard it as no longer a mystery.

35

You will never know the Great Mystery,
       but, I can tell you a little of it.

In many other cultures, it is described by what it <u>isn't</u>,
       that is one way of defining something,
       but look how misleading this can be.

       We say that the water is not dry,
       and yet, there is water in the air we breathe,
       and ice on the river is water.

       We say the fire is not cold,
       but the sticks which you brought here tonight were.
       Do not the sticks contain the fire?

       Ah, you say only the promise of the fire.

       Then perhaps it is that way with us,
       we contain the promise of the Great Mystery.

       Perhaps in some ways, we are the Great Mystery, and it is shared by all of us.

To some people,
       they call it the spirit that is inside of them;
       many do not even know it is inside them,
       that is the link to the Great Mystery.

YOU ARE a tool, a promise, a great joy. Think on this.

It is cold. Snowflakes are falling.
       Yet, look out on the field.
       Close your eyes,
       and think on the field in the summertime:
       picture corn stalks, squash blossoms, beans. . .
       Are they not real?
       Do you not know inside, that they will be there?
       If you do know it, is it not there already?

You say you need comfort,
       not from the cold outside, but the cold that is inside.
       It is a fact that I can warm your body,
       but only you can warm your heart.

It is true that there are great burdens. . .
      We all have burdens. . .
      Living is itself a burden.

There's the old man who could hardly go on.
      His eyes were weak, and he went hunting for the deer,
      but he could not follow the tracks,
      and he grew hungrier and hungrier
      and weaker and weaker.

The deer followed him for many miles,
      and finally the deer took pity
      and came up to the old man and said to him,
      "Look at me. I am here.
      Use your bow and arrow,
      and when you have killed me,
      take me back to your village
      so your family and friends can eat."

The old Indian sat on the snow, and thought on this.
      "No, I cannot kill you and take you back with me.
      You are too kind and generous;
      to give yourself is the greatest gift of all.
      It is obvious that you are the Great Spirit,
          the Great Mystery."

The deer stood over the old Indian and said,
      "You are very wise. Follow me."
      And he went into a cave that was filled with jars of beans and corn,
      and the deer said for the man to eat what he needed,
      and said to take what was needed to the village,
      then leave the rest for the next hunter wise enough to respect life.

He carried a great load of beans and corn back to his village, and fed his people.

Then, he asked the shaman to do the deer dance,
      and the shaman said, "I can't; I haven't eaten the deer.
      The deer dance is for the feast of the deer."

The old Indian said,
      "We have only eaten well because of the deer,
      and that was part of the Great Mystery."

The shaman agreed, and tied the bells on his ankles,
     and the old man gathered the juniper branches
     and stuck juniper antlers in his headband
     and led the dance of the deer.
Because everyone had been well fed,
     the dance---- was---- good. (Whispered very deliberately.)

Often times, what we seek is not what we are given;
     this is because the Great Spirit,
     the Great Mystery is wiser than us.
     Sometimes, I think it is because the Great Mystery makes a good joke.

Can you tell me anything of yourself tonight?
Nothing to tell.
But I appreciate you, and would like to know you better.
That can never be.
As much as we can know of each other,
we never know but a speck of what each is,
     for what we are is part of the Great Mystery
              that can't be known, and still be a mystery.

Don't fear, because you don't understand.

What about Hank, whose voice you use? Do you have a word for him?
Everything I say is for anyone who listens.
     The fire only warms those who come close to it,
     and only comforts those who seek it.

Where are you from? What time and place?
Time and place are immaterial;
     they are fluid- -
     one can come from many times and places.

Are you male or female?
What would it matter?

I'm trying to know you better for Hank.
     He is sometimes frightened that you teach much through him.

There is nothing to be frightened about.

Are you in his imagination,
or coming from somewhere else,
choosing him as a receptive soul to speak through?

Many of us are a part of each other.

Do not ask that which you really do not want to know.
What is imagination, anyway?
What is wisdom?
What is ignorance?

Are they all both spiritual and cognitive functions?

All are part of the Great Mystery.

Is it safe to assume. . .
It is never safe to assume!

To rephrase,
can we know that you come from the Great Mystery,
rather than the Great Evil?

Only you can open your heart to learn more of the Great Mystery,
and only when you and the Great Mystery are both ready, will you know more.

As for the "great evil" as you call it,
that is why we have light,
for light doesn't comfort the great evil.

"Great evil" is the ignorance that resides within us.

"Great evil" has many names:
to some, hatred; some, greed;
some would call the "great evil" lust,
some ignorance;
these are our reflections,
but understand,
we are not children of evil,
we are children of good.

Think about the word "good"--one more letter than God.
Think on it.

Hank will be frustrated by no explanation in the morning, as I am by not understanding now.

(Said with a smile,) Hank must think on it, too.

I will tell you this- -
      when you fear evil, you let it exist.

When you face it,
      with courage and wisdom and faith,
      it shrinks away to nothing.

Evil is so easily destroyed.

Would you put some more sticks on the fire, please?

The Questions
January 17, 1998

(He seems short of breath tonight.)
There is so much more you need to know--
There is so much more I need to tell you--

Visit me by the fire
     and find warmth in my words,
     and comfort in my ideas

     as I will find warmth in your words
     and comfort in your ideas.

I am old, and have gained the wisdom to know that we are all each other's teacher;
     we are all students.

Do not be afraid to question,
     especially do not be afraid to question yourself.

Questioning yourself is like watering the corn,
     it permits growth, makes possible the fruit.

Don't seek to blame others,
Don't seek to curse the demons.

I have learned in my years that the real devil is confusion,
     the real strength is in love;
     but they are both inside us.

(After a prolonged pause, I asked, "Is it time to say goodnight, or have you more to teach?")

We have enough to think on--
     to think too many thoughts at once is to invite the confusion,
     to become lost in the chaos.

To seek to understand, one step at a time,
     is the pathway to peace, understanding, and love.

(Hank rolled over, and as he woke up, he said, "I don't think he is well. How would I know that?" As of March 14, we have not heard from the Old Indian again, and miss him.)

Missing Our Friend, the Old Indian

by Tomi, during one of his long absences

As the rain falls down upon our roof,
      I think back to the warmth and wisdom of the fires we shared.
And I miss your way with words,
      and insights, timely made.
You blessed our lives for months
      with visits when we needed your help
          to make sense of death and life.

And we wonder where you've gone,
      and if you're feeling well,
      or if you've crossed some line, to a better, brighter time.

Questions still confuse me, just as you knew they would--
Hank still feels your comfort, as the guide helps heal his pain.
You gave us God's own guidance, signs from God's gracious hand.
We want to say "thank you," for you were part of God's own plan.

If we hear from you again, it will be a reunion fine--
      but if the connection now is gone,
      we still know it to have been a gift;
We hope for a future meeting with you, somewhere, some time.

Thank you for all your stories and teachings and conversation,
      wisdom always phrased just right.
May God's love enfold you on this cold, dark night,
      and bless you now and forever, as you walk in Holy Light.

The Circle of Time
The Old Indian's Return

March 30, 1998

I miss my music;
     and the scent of juniper.

Would you sit, and share bread with an old man?

(chuckling) I have been to the fair, and I saw something interesting.
     I will share it with you.

In the fair, they have horses that go around in a circle,
     and they think it is fun to see the same thing over and over.

Would it not be more fun, to take these ponies,
     and ride over hills they haven't seen before?

I wonder at these Belagaana.
All these mysteries, and they still, still have so little understanding.

I think they have no imagination,
     but I will tell you a little about imaginations.

The scientist tries to find an explanation for your imagination.
The scientist tries to explain everything;
     that's, that's because the scientist is insecure;
     See, insecure people know that the only real power is wisdom,
     so they seek wisdom, and
     they don't understand that the knowing comes from inside,
     that is what lives in the mind and the heart.

And so the Belagaana scientist can only accept what he can see, what he can prove,
     and not what he can feel.

Our ancestors in the long ago yesterdays
     knew within their minds what was necessary to know.
They knew it by what we call instinct in animals.
     But this is a foolish concept, too.

Why is it we as humans have wisdom, (pounding his chest,)
  but the animals only have instinct. (Said sarcastically.)

Perhaps I read them wrong,
  and the human is so insecure,
  that he mourns his lack of instinct,
  and is jealous of all the animals that are more knowing.

They tell you, it is inherited within us,
  it is passed from mother to child, much of what is known,
  Look, the important knowing,
  and what we do not inherit at birth, we can ...by our elders.

The assumption that one is better than another
  because they know more is a lie.

Think on this...who is better suited here in this desert,
  your family and friends in the Pueblo,
who know how to live in harmony with the cactus, and the wrens, the birds and the rabbits,

or the Belagaana who must build an artificial ------,
  find water from deep within the Mother,
  shading themselves from the Father Sun?

And trying so vainly to grow what the Great Spirit never intended. Think on this.

Which is the greater wisdom; the one who can adapt and cope,
  or the one who has to create his artificial existence?
  And live literally in his own cage?

But I am digressing, I was talking about the carousel,
  and the horses who go round and around and go nowhere.

And I think in many ways perhaps, this is the Belagaana's searching for the purpose,
  the continuity,
  by revolving, to capture time,
  the Belagaana have trouble with time.(whispered)
    It's because they spend it like money,
    they borrow on their future time.

We know time is the great cycle,
  and that ultimately we are all riding the carousel,
  the carousel of time, and is it not truly a merry go round?

We have talked much of time before.

But I ask you, do you think that carousels create questions?

And in the great cycle of time,
　　　don't the answers appear again and again?

In the end, are these not the clues the Great Mystery gives us?

Are these not what makes life so exciting?

Time is not a set of stairs to climb, that ultimately gets somewhere...
　　　Time is the cycle, the circle, the great circle of existence.

Sometimes we work too hard,
　　　why do we work so hard?
I wish I knew.

Perhaps the answers are somewhere in the cycle,
　　　perhaps we are on the edge of the discovery again,
　　　　　that we don't need to work so hard.

That we need to live more.

　　　Think on this:
　　　Every civilization that has ever built great monuments to itself,
　　　　　has only built great tombstones to itself.

　　　The pyramids are the great tombstones of Egypt,
　　　Teotihuacan is the great tombstone of the Mayans,
　　　Mesa Verde and Chaco Canyon are the tombstones of our ancestors.

The peoples who do not build great monuments, continue to live good lives.
　　　Think on this.

And have some more bread. It is good.

You ask why I have been gone so long.
I told you before; I have great journeys I have to take.
Do you think I can only talk to you?
No, but we want you to know we missed you.

Well, I have missed you, too.

But, you need to understand, your spirit guide,
　　　　even when I am not here, your spirit guide is.
　　　　All you have to do is seek it.

And don't only look for your spirit guide when you need something;
　　　　look to your spirit guide when you want to share good news,
　　　　　　　　when you want to share great joy;
　　　　　　　　invite your spirit guide to your fire.

You are welcome at our fire always. We are honored when you come to visit.

And you are always welcome at my fire;
　　　　the next time, I will have some stories for you.

I hope that is soon.

I will be here for awhile.
I must confess that I am not as young as I used to be,
　　　　that sometimes the journeys I take are more difficult,
　　　　and sometimes, to see the visions,
　　　　takes much out of me. But do not worry, I will be here.

I thank you for sharing my fire and my bread. Will you play the flute?

I understand that you have missed your music, and the smell of juniper branches.

Much. *So have we.*

The music speaks to the soul, the music is the language of the soul,
　　　　not just of our people, but of all peoples.
　　　　There is no people so poor, that they don't have music.

(I lit some juniper incense, and played a CD of Native American flute and drum music. Hank woke briefly, but we have found that if I tell him about the visit, he has no memories of our conversation by the next morning. So I tell him about it again then, and sometimes play the tape of the visit. But it bothers him to hear such a different voice coming from his mouth. Sometimes he even has difficulty understanding what has been said. So now I try to transcribe the tape onto computer that same night while my memory is fresh, for sometimes his words are so soft, that it is the gesture that helps me know what he is saying. By following along with the print version, Hank can understand, and sometimes fill in the words that I have missed.)

Stories of the Long, Long Ago People
April 5, 1998

Hola, mi amigo. See, you can teach this old dog new tricks.
　　　Sometime, I can learn another whole language.
 It was the way of our people long ago, to speak many languages.
　　　On the plaza of our cities, you would hear many different languages.
　　　We had to; we traded with many different people.

You had asked me, a long time ago, I think, about the kiva,
　　　and why was the hole in it.
　　　And I don't think I answered you.
　　　It was a good question and is not a secret,
　　　　　although we do have many secrets that we will not tell you.
The sipapu was a reminder to us of the darkness out of which we came.

It is our belief-- you say our myth, you always say someone else's beliefs are myths--
　　　it is our belief that mankind rose through four levels of the underground
　　　to get to where we are today.

In the third level, we lived a very simple life,
　　　and we could talk to the animals, and they could talk to us.

It was dark all of the time, not night dark, just like a rainy day.
And the rains came, and the rain came, and places we lived, they filled with water.
And we climbed the hillsides, to the place where the giant reeds grow,
　　　and two people cut a hole in the giant reed,
　　　and they helped the animals inside;
　　　each animal brought its gift.

The turkey was the last to make its way.
　　　It was laden down with the seeds for every plant to be grown.
And the two people helped the turkey into the reed just as the water got to it,
　　　and they climbed the reed as fast as they could.

And they came out of this hole in the earth, into the sunshine we have today.
　　　And they saw this and said, "It is good."
　　　　That was how first man and first woman got here.

The flooding came through the reed, and filled the great lake.
     And first man and first woman walked through the sand to the lake,
     and they named all the fish,
     and in the great lake, there were great fish they called whales.

And they planted the seeds that turkey had carried.

And it was dark when the sun went away,
     and first man and first woman climbed up on top of the mountain,
     and called to the Great Spirit,
     "Oh, Great Spirit, it is so dark, and we are afraid."

And the Great Spirit threw a handful of shells on the sand, and said,
     "Put these in the sky, they will be light for you;
        when the sun is on the other side."

Coyote came to first man and first woman and said,
     "You saved me from the flood, let me do something for you.
        I know I can jump high; I will put the stars in the sky for you."

Coyote did this,
     and he took the biggest of the abalone shells,
     and made it the moon, and placed it,
     and he was climbing the ladder to place the other stars,
     and he started to fall.
        But he threw the other stars, and they scattered all over the sky,
        and that is why even today the stars are so scattered--
        it was Coyote, coyote who tries so hard,
        but sometimes falls so short.

It was the story of the hole from which we emerged, to the light of day.
     This is how we escaped the great flood.

Another story that the Navajo tells is that they lived in the mud,
     in the underworld,
     and they climbed the ladder to get out of the mud,
     to come into the world of sunshine.

Different groups have different stories of their origins;
     I like to think that ours is true, and yours is myth, but you think otherwise. That's OK.

The Navajo did not know how to grow corn or cotton or beans.
     We taught them, and gave them seed. There is a story about that.

The Navajo used to watch us plant our corn.
     And when it was ripe, they'd come and steal some.

So one time when it was corn planting time, we invited the Navajo to our village.
     And we said, "Why don't you help us with the corn planting dance,
          and then we will teach you how to plant the corn?"

And they danced, and they sang with us,
        and in the morning, we took them out into the field,
        and showed them how we planted the corn,
        and how the men of the village would take their turns
        spilling their seed on the ground to make it fertile for the corn.

And the Navajo took the seed, they went back to their camp,
     and they said,
     "This will not do; for if we plant the corn and we wander;
     we will have to build houses like the city people, and stay in one place."
        So they started to do this, but still they would raid.

They raided until the Spanish came.
     The Spanish gave them sheep,
        and you can not raid when you have to watch sheep.

They gave them the great gift of weaving;
     and the Navajo weaved beautiful blankets that told great stories.

And that is how the Navajo became peaceful.
     We gave them corn, and the Spanish gave them sheep,
        They ate the corn, and spun the sheep's wool into thread,
           which they wove into blankets, and became peaceful.

Maybe the Belagaana should learn how to weave blankets.
     This is a joke, don't you think?

I am an old man, and telling these stories to you has tired me.
    But come, sit on the hillside with me, look down into the valley,
    look on our fields of corn and beans;
    if you look closely, you can see the squash growing large and ripening.

Do you know that the center out of the squash blossom is the symbol of fertility,
        and that is why when a young girl becomes a woman,
        she is given the squash blossom necklace.
    See, the squash blossom is the womb of the flower, the womb of the plant,
        and from it the squash children come.
    The squash is the womb of the plant, this is another of our traditions.

Sit, feel the breeze, and watch the corn grow.

I have a question, if not for tonight, for another time.
    A question from Hank. He was wondering . . .
    I know him!

Yes, you speak through him sometimes.
    He is good.

What he is wondering about right now is how people made the transition from being hunters and gatherers, to being people of crops, who plant and stay in one place. I think you have talked a little of that tonight, with the Navajo; is there any other wisdom you can share with him?

Well, it takes a special place.
You see, our people long long ago, would gather the pods of the yucca,
    or dig their roots or the roots of the ___, or__
    and then the women of the tribe said they were tired,
     and they needed to rest by the water, and let their babies grow.

And the men said they could rest by the water,
    they also ate all of the food that is there,
    and the women said, the food grows better by the water,
    and if we pray, maybe we can make it grow better yet.

This is the way the corn planting dance started,
    and this is the way the squash dance started,
        because our dances are prayers;
    this is the way that we talk to the Great Mystery.

But, understand what happened.

While the long ago people planted the seeds,
       and then it would take a season for the seeds to grow,
       after they had rested from their planting, they journeyed.

In the spring they would journey up into the mountains;
       and in the winter or in the fall they would come back down into the valley by the river.
          And when they came back to the valley,
              then there were beans, and there was squash,
              and they could stay in the valley for the winter,
              and not be hungry.

After years of doing this, they said,
       "If we stayed by the river, instead of going into the mountains,
       we could make certain the squash and the beans and the chilies and corn
       and other crops got water and they would grow better
       and we would have more food for the winter.
          And none of our babies would starve,
          and our elders could sit by the warm fire and smoke the tobacco,
          and they would no longer have to gather dried berries in the snow."
          And this is the way that we learned to farm.

This is interesting,
that while the long ago people stopped by the rivers to weave sandals out of the river grass,
       they learned how to plant the seeds.
       The secret ___ was the fact that the long ago people did not go barefoot,
          but wore sandals made of river grass.
       The scientists find the stone points and tools and for some strange reason,
          think these tools were used for killing;
               some were,
          but some were used to prepare food, to chop wood,
              to cut the trees we used to make our houses,
          others were used to strip the bark that was used for medicine.

       And to make our containers and pots, there were tools used to dig the clay.
       They weren't all weapons, they weren't all to kill.

       The key is in the sandals.

How were the sandals the key? I am not sure I understand.

When the scientists find the sandals,
they will understand that the long ago people were peaceful people
       that sought comfort and had the wisdom to weave and work with fibers.

The sandals even of the long long ago people were painted, and dyed;
don't you see, beauty was important to them.

There's a story that after the underworld,
the people and the animals spoke to each other through song,
and is not song the most beautiful way to use our voice?

Music was the way to communicate,
before we had birds, we had music.

Look about you, do not the birds have music, too,
does not the coyote sing to the moon at night?

Long ago people enjoyed the dance, sang the songs, made the music,
made even the sandals on their feet a thing of art.

As they learned to grow their crops,
they painted their toenails, they painted their faces, they wore earrings.

Do you understand?
I think so. Hank will be very pleased with what you have told.

Does this answer your question?
Somewhat, I don't know how they left hunting behind,
but I understand that it was to feed their babies, that they became the farmers.

They not only hunted animals,
they hunted the fruits, the berries, the roots, the barks, ___and the herbs.

These people of long long ago knew so many of the medicines
(I changed the tape, and took too long to get some of this.)

They knew to follow the animals to find the things that they needed.
The squirrel would gather the nuts,
and the long ago people would follow the squirrel.
Other animals would know where the water was,
and they would follow the animal to the water.
They would follow the bees to their hive for the honey.

These people couldn't go to the Piggly Wiggly;
remember also that long long ago, the land was not as dry as today,
there was more food and animals, so they ate well.

They also fished, it is interesting how they would fish.
     They would make baskets out of the river willow
     and they would gather all of the fish together, driving them into a pool,
         and just simply lift them out by the basketful.
     Then they would dry them.
They would have fish in the long nights of winter.

It was much easier to catch a fish, than a deer, even in the desert.

I hope these stories help you.
They do, and I thank you very much.

You are welcome. Now let us be quiet, and watch the corn grow.

(Long pause here when Hank rolled over to go to sleep, then rolled back for a last comment.)

     The first crop was not corn---corn came much later. The beans were first, then the squash. Corn was a grass in Mexico, called teosinte. It still grows in Chiapas. Wouldn't it be fun to have the Grandmother Corn to show our children? I would like that.

(I notice a language pattern in rereading the stories he tells; in the oral tradition, sentences and phrases frequently begin with the word "and." It reminded me of studying ancient Greek, which frequently uses the word transliterated "kai," which means either "and" or "but," to connect the telling of the stories of scripture. These stories are all meant to be heard, rather than read.

While working on our book *Global Gardening* that is on food used for survival all over the world, we grew many plants from all over. One of our favorites was the teosinte. And regarding the last comment he made, when I was growing up in North Dakota, for several years in the autumn I was among the young people who helped a truck farmer harvest corn for market, and in the spring helped plant tomatoes and melons. During my time in his fields, it was true, I really could hear the corn grow.)

The Spirit Dolls

From my husband's dream, April 24, 1998
as recalled by Hank Bruce

The dream began, or at least my recollection of it did, with an Indian family visiting a large city. I think it was Albuquerque and the sense is that these were Pueblo people. There are flashes of musicians in a park or perhaps it was a fairgrounds or festival. The sound of country guitars blends with that of a Mariachi band. A Caribbean steel drum band, like the one that used to be across from the Pirates ride at Disney World contrasts with a harpist performing Saint-Saens in the shade of a cottonwood. The members of this family and all the others present applaud, but it is more that they are keeping time with the assorted music. The audience is being drawn into the bands. Through this communion they all become one. It is a form of communication that transcends language, goes beyond culture.

The children are small and this all seems new to them. They constantly ask questions but it all sounds like babble. I can't understand what they are saying. The adults tell them to wait until they get home. Then they should ask, a name was spoken but I can't remember it.

The next image is of a Pueblo festival dance. There are tourists in all sizes, colors and dress watching as the clowns and Katchinas emerge from the various buildings and gather in the plaza where there are tables of food, pottery and assorted arts. It is getting dark and cold. Fires are lit, many small ones and one large one in the center of the plaza. People are sitting on lawn chairs on the Pueblo roofs. There is chanting and the heavy beat of drums. A flute is played by a figure in a purple and yellow outfit. He is hunched over, Kokopeli like. He leads all the women of the village in a dance around the central fire. He disappears; the women all disperse; and the Clown leaps into the center of the plaza. All of the Katchinas follow, then the elders of the community dance and chant. Soon all the Indians and most of the tourists are also dancing and entering into the chants.

The children are tired from the dancing and they literally collapse at the feet of an old man. There are Anglo children, Black children, Orientals, bright-eyed Chicanos and others with the Indian children. The old man puts down his flute and sits cross legged as the children form a semi-circle around him. They begin to ask questions, but he raises his hand to silence them. His face is in shadows so I never did get a clear image of him. As best I can recall from my dreamtime this is what followed.

The children ask questions about how and why they are different. The Old Indian opens his canvas bag and pulls out a bouquet of flowers. "Is this not beautiful?"
They all nod and say yes.
He begins to remove first the cheerful sunflowers; then the fragrant roses. The dark blue penstemon are also plucked from his hand. Soon all that is left are several sprigs of pungent chamisa. "When the Great Mystery plants a garden, do not many kinds of flowers grow?"

They all nod in agreement.

"Each of these flowers," he gestures toward the varied colors, fragrances and floral forms arrayed before them, "is beautiful in its own existence, but are they not far more beautiful when they are gathered together so that they can compliment their companions?"

The flowers are distributed among the children. The feasting and dancing continue as the flames diminish and the plaza becomes shades darker.

Finally the Old Indian reaches into his canvas bag and removes a cornhusk doll dressed in the traditional costume of a Pueblo Indian woman. Next he pulls forth a Cowboy doll, then a cornhusk version of a Mariachi doll. He continues to take dolls from the bag until there are dozens spread across the dirt at his feet.

"The colors and cut of these clothes speak to you of their cultures. Do they not?" He points to several, then waves his hand across the rest of them.

The children are gleefully pointing to the dolls that represent their culture. Then try to identify some of the other ones.

The Old Indian raises his hand and motions for silence, "But look on this," he waves his hands over the bouquet of dolls and there is a haze that conceals them all.

When this haze clears, all the clothes are gone and all the corn husk dolls look much the same.

"They all look the same. I can't tell which one was mine." several of the children spoke in unison.

"Do you not see the lesson here?"

The children are all silent for many seconds.

"Does this mean that inside we are all the same?" one of the children hesitantly asks.

The Old Indian clapped his hands, "Yes. You have learned a great truth tonight."

He waved his hands again and the dress was restored to the cornhusk dolls. Each child took one. The Old Indian raised his flute again and the flames retreated into the glowing coals.

The Rites of Purification
April 27, 1998

(Because I was facing a medical test the next day, I was going without food--which proved impossible for this diabetic, so the test was eventually canceled. Hank, meanwhile, was in the bathtub, leaning back, with a candle lit, and native flute music playing. Then he slowly raised his right hand, with the index finger extended, a gesture that I have come to associate with a sleep talk episode about to begin. Then, with his left hand cupped, he brought water up and poured it over his head and face, and wiped his brow. It reminded me of an action one might see in a sauna. So, I ran for the paper and pen, to record what follows.)

It is time...
  Time to ask you, my friends
  What do you know of purification?
  What do you understand of our two avenues
    to restoration of harmony?

I will tell you something of our ways,
  so when you are the elders, you will be able to instruct others.

Think on this, but do not answer.

We all admit that we need purification...
  That is why we came to the sweat lodge;
  that is why we fast.

I know other people in other places
  and other times of tomorrow and yesterday
  also seek to purify their body and their soul and their mind.

Let us first look at our people.

Like a stone cast into the ocean, that makes a ripple that never ends,
  each person in infinitely important.

Every other person is also like a stone cast into the ocean,
  sending out ripples; each equally significant and insignificant.

56

When we stand on a mountain top after a fast,
      we can look east, and see tomorrow;
      we can look west, and see yesterday.
      Such is the power of the fast.

When we are seeking our harmony,
      when we are out of harmony, we are not pure.

(Laughing)
 We'll never be pure, that's right.

The Great Mystery made us that way, to laugh at, perhaps,
      never completely pure.

But the Great Mystery gave us signs of what purity is.

In the sweat lodge,
      we feel the steam rising, we smell the juniper smoke,
            And poisons of hate and distrust
            and anger and jealousy pour out of us,
            and we are left cleansed and closer to harmony.

As the steam rises and drips from our hair,
      as we chant the chants,
      as we splash water on the stones and make the steam rise to us,
      we have the signs from the Great Mystery, of what purity is.

Some no longer go to the sweat lodge,
      some think they can replenish self
            with that which is found in a bottle.

      NO. Your spirit is not replenished in that way.

When you watch the sun rise,
      When you drink cool water of the stream,
            When the steam rises and drips from your hair,
                  When you smell the juniper smoke,
                     When you chant the chants,

      These are connections between you and the Great Spirit.
      These are the signs Great Spirit gives you.

These are the reasons we go into the darkness of sweat lodge;
        when you close your eyes,
        and are there, naked, saturated with you own impurities,
        your mind and spirit see what is good,
                and you connect with it.

When you have sat until smoke no longer can be inhaled,
        and steam no longer rises, when water is splashed on the rocks,
                then you go to the river to bathe;
                you are closer to harmony.

In another culture, the Hindus bathe in the river called Ganges,
        which they call a holy river;
                to us, all rivers are holy.

Sweat lodge is one way to purify.

The other is fasting.

It is curious that in many of life's most difficult times, we fast.

We call this very Indian, but it is not, it is more universal.
The ones called Mormons,
        who came long ago and settled in the Four Corners area,
        would fast when facing a difficult decision,
        or when they erred, were out of harmony, a condition they call sin.

The sisters who arrived with the priests, and helped set up missions
        fasted one day a week;
        they didn't understand why,
        but knew it helped to communicate better with the Great Mystery.

We often think of fasting as denial;
        we will not take food, even if our stomach growls,
        we think of it as sacrificing.

Fasting doesn't force us to focus on our physical hunger.

Fasting liberates the mind to think,
        to communicate with the Great Mystery.

We often fast in solitude.

Many religions fast...
     Muslims fast, to purify;
     Buddhists fast, to purify and move closer to harmony;
     Hindus fast, to find Nirvana.

Can we all be wrong?

Think on this as we talk of purifying ourselves.

Some of you will choose the sweat lodge for one day,
     and it actually is ours.

Others of you will choose the fast, for a day, two or three days.
     As you go through the fast,
     you will receive the gift of the vision; it is not to be feared.
          With the fast, you will come closer to the Great Mystery,
          who gives the vision which will effect the rest of your life.

Think on it.

Some of you who lack the courage
     will seek comfort and relief in the bottles and bars
          and destroy yourself--
     DO NOT do this.

Find the courage to suffer a little to find the harmony,
     for your life and more.

We will go into the kiva and chant, and you will make the decisions.

Come, I will lead the way.

The Scientists' Folly

late May or early June, 1998

It was in those days long ago, that we spoke to the plants.
    And they spoke to us.

You see, in those days long ago,
    the spirits of the plants could talk to the spirits of the peoples.
    And they told us much knowledge.

And that is how we learned not only what was good to eat and what was not,
    but what was medicine, and what was not.

I would like to tell you of the folly of the scientists.

Of when they come to study the people of the tribes,
    they say that, because their understanding was so limited,
    the people of the tribes were inferior because their language was so limited.

The truth of it is that the language of the tribes is not limited
    but that the scientists failed to understand what was being spoken to them,
    so they called the people of the tribes ignorant.

Language of tribal peoples was very rich.
    And often times, inflection of a word gave it a secondary meaning.

They also thought that the people of the tribe were superstitious, and they know this is false.
    They worshiped ___ than these people,

they knew that the people of the tribes, and yet,
    they, worshiped so many gods,
    they couldn't remember them.
    They called them Santos;
        and again, they were close to the truth, without understanding of it.

They didn't realize that the power of the Great Mystery is in everything,
    and therefore there is a unity in anything and everything.

They thought that they were superstitious and had all of the herbs that were religious,
    and that we had to do the chants to invoke the gods.

And yet, if you go to one of these healers of theirs today,
  they will chant the strange sounding words that nobody can understand,
    and they give you incantations,
  and they give you little magic pills that are supposed to make you well.

How foolish to call us superstitious!
They didn't understand that we knew that there were two kinds of healing;
  the first was the healing of the body;

  and for this, we studied the symptoms, and we think on this;
    so little understanding.

One had a fever,
  and they said he was possessed with demons,
    and they called us primitive!

I would see someone with a fever,
   and with my language, Tiwa, [or Tewa?]
      we had 27 different words to describe a fever.

That's how we knew the symptoms;
  that's how we knew what to treat it with.
  And we treated it with our medicines.

But there was a second kind of medicine;
  that was to heal the spirit.
  And for that, we sang songs; we played the drum.
  We shook the rattle.

We did this to tell the one who was sick,
  that he had the power to overcome this illness,
  and again,
  when one was sick,
  we tried to heal the body and the spirit together.
      Does this not make sense?

The tribes did not ....(hard to understand)

In one of the long agos before,
  we were happy and we did not labor.

We gathered what we needed,
  and then we sang the happy songs around the campfire.

We discovered our art, and we visioned great stories.

And then, with the relentless march of greed,
     and the lust for power and control,
    the plants they came forth from the fields and the forest,
    and they domesticated mankind.

(Chuckling;) Look at the folly of the scientists.

    It was vain enough to think that it was humanity who domesticated wheat,
        look at the evidence.
    The wheat could never have spread like it did, without using mankind.
        We did not domesticate the grain, and the fruit, and the roots;
            they domesticated us.
    They talked us into their slaves;
        they taught us how to carry water to them, how to plant them,
        how to fight their enemies for them.
    They taught us to carry their seed all over the world.

Think on this.

We did not transform wild rice and maize and squash and beans and carrots and cabbages;
    think of the legend of the Jonathan Appleseed.

The apple tree taught this man to wander through the eastern states, planting its seed.

And where he planted its seed, they brought other men to tend great orchards.
    The apple tree was very wise.
        Yes, even today, many of us are still slaves to these plants.

Come miss, and watch the sun rise.

Here, I will share with you my corn pollen.
    Take a pinch; scatter it to the morning breeze,
    as the sun breaks over the mountain side.
    This is the tribute we pay to our moss master the bees plant.
        [At least, that is what the phrase sounded like to me.]

In the Belagaana book they talk of farming as being a curse.
    There is some truth to that.

(Very weakly whispers this part.)
Would you help me to my feet, so that I may great the dawn with respect?

Thank the Great Mystery for another day.

It is cold this morning.

I am thankful that you are here. This is good.

(He chants, with the microphone raised like a rattle or shaker)
At-ta-ha-hi-ees   Or-da-hol at-ta-hi-ee as-a-ha-ah-sha-ha-da

The day....is....good. (Spoken softly.)

(Hank does not sing, so to hear him chant was quite a surprise. We wonder at the words he used, if they have a meaning known to others. And we were both concerned at the diminishing strength we hear in our friend's voice.)

The Sacred Cedar Tree

June 13, 1998

(As he begins talking, he is barely whispering;
       it becomes obvious that he is very weak tonight,
       as though near unto death.)

Are you ready?
I will need for you to shred the bark.
       Do you know what this is?
       This is the bark of the cedar; this is a holy tree.
              It is the tree of the Great Mystery. We will do the healing chant.

I need for you to shred the bark. Then, we will go to the fire.
       And I will teach you the ceremony.

In the long ago time, many agos past, many cycles of time,
       the cedar tree could talk to us, and we to it.
              Now, we don't believe that the tree could talk, so we don't hear it.

Long ago, the story goes,
       the great leader was troubled that his people did not know good from evil.
       And he went out onto the mountainside to talk to the Great Mystery.

And the Great Mystery told him that his people must purify their thoughts
       with the bark and the wood of the red cedar.

There are two cedars; the red cedar which has red wood and a clean smell;
              it is the scent that cleanses and purifies.
       Many bird houses today are built of cedar, as are the wish boxes of the Belagaana;
              the Belagaana girls have chests built that they put their wishes in.
                     It is a nice custom, don't you think?

They see the beauty of the tree through a dark glass.
       They do not fully understand that it is a sacred tree.
       But they still honor it; that is good.

We should not be critical of the Belagaana, because of their ignorance.
       They try.

Sit, and let me put some more branches on the fire.

64

Have you got the bark shredded?

Good.

We will fill this pan with water, and drop the shredded bark in. Also the berries.
     While we are waiting for the tea to brew, we will show you how the cedar,
     which some may call the __ variety,

(I asked him to repeat what variety, but he only has the strength to tell me once this night, and if I
miss it, he simply goes on.)

Take these twigs, and hold them in the fire,
     until they are burned just a little bit; and you have charcoal.
     My hands are too old, I cannot hold the sticks in there;
     the pain of age is in my hands.

When you have some charcoal on the stick, ah, that is good,
     don't try to burn it too much.
Take the stick, make the marks of respect on your forehead; the three lines.
We make these marks to tell the Great Mystery that we seek its help in our health.

The seeds of the cedar are used to make the Belagaana drink of ginger [gin, sic].
     Gin was named for the Dutch word for juniper;
and the red cedar is known by the Belagaana scientists as Juniperus communis.

It is known by our people as gad or gatz.
     The berries were used by the Hopi people, and the Zunis, a long time ago,
        to help the woman who was having a baby. It speeded the birth.
     The Navajo and the Chicanos used the juniper to make an abortion.

Then we take this tea we have brewed, and we each drink of it;
     it will heal and purify.
Put the shredded bark into the flames in the corner of the fire.
     Lean forward now, wave the smoke over your face; rub it into your hair.
     Breathe the smoke; it is the smoke of the holy tree.
        Do you not feel cleaner now, purer?

When you are old, you will need to do this often.
     Take the charcoal and rub it on my wrist. Thank you.

        Some day, you will be the shaman,
        and you will have to teach others the mystery of our sacred tree.

Now, we know that to drink the tea is a healthy thing.
    I think your tea is ready. Please help me to hold my cup.

    I seem to be very weak tonight. Perhaps this tea will help. Thank you.

Drinking this tea will help my body's blood to go on the journey.
    Let me inhale the smoke of the juniper one more time. Nnnn.

    Help me to my feet, please. Let me steady myself on your arm.
    That's much better; thank you.

    Oh, do not worry, I will be fine.

I will care for you anyway, or the Great Mystery will care for you.

Thank you. Would you do the chant of thanks?
This is one of the first chants that a shaman must learn,
    because we have so much to be thankful for.
    Would you do that chant for me? Thank you.

I hummed a hymn of thanksgiving, "We Give Thee But Thine Own, Whatever the Gift May Be;
All That We Have Is Thine Alone, A Trust O Lord from Thee" and he rested a bit.

ENOUGH!
    ENOUGH of the long faces!
    Did you not drink the tea?
    Did you not feel strengthened and warmed?
        Then why do you look so sad?
            I have told you of the cedar; of how it one time talked to us;
            do you not understand that as a shaman, it still talks to us?

Do you not hear the message as you hold these twigs;
        do you not feel the message,
        do you not feel the life?

These things you must do, if you are a shaman;
        anyone can go and pick berries. Any fool. Any child.

Did you thank the tree for its twigs?
    Did you thank the tree for its seeds? Its needles?

You must be still;
    breathe the smoke;
        make pure your thought; some would call it meditation.

Our ancient ones knew; they all understood; they were all shamans.
    They understood talking to the tree.
    They understood how the tree answers.

Do you think that the only way we can talk is with our mouths?

    Stand here before this tree.
    Close your eyes and open your mind.
    What do you feel? Open your mind further, and further.
    These things you must practice. I cannot give you these things.
        You have to find them for yourself.

(After this, we wondered if he was still alive, somewhere in the Southwest, or if he had lived in another time, only to visit us. He left us with many questions. My biggest concern was that I saw Hank's own health deteriorating, due to difficulty breathing, with enormous forest fires near by. In his heart, I knew that he wanted to be home writing, rather than continuing with other employment. My deepest fear was that I might lose both Hank and the Old Indian at the same time.)

Substance & Beauty
September 8, 1998

(As he began, the words sounded like "therropen terlittle," then:)
Will you walk with me for a minute?

We have not talked together for a long time.

It has been a long time, and I have missed you. Welcome.

Thank you. It is good to be back.
I have been so far away.

Shall we walk over to the arroyo and watch the sun set?

Yes. How are you feeling? When last we talked, you were not well.

I have rested much.

Would you hand me my cane, please? Thank you.

I am not as young as I once was in this cycle;
and sometimes our age is not subtle when it reminds us.

It is a beautiful evening, but the chill is heavy in the air,

If we look to the east, the moon is impatient to be on its journey.
If we look there, beside it, it is beside the moon, there are the two stars.
They're brothers who do not know each other,
        because the moon has been between them.

When they were young, when they were only children,
        they were separated,
        and each was taken as a prisoner to other lands,
        so they did not know each other.

And they did not know the ways of their people.

And then, then, when they came again to trade,
    at the villages of the Salt River,
    they met, one from the north with buffalo hides,
    and one from the south with feathers of the parrot, blue and green.

It is interesting that the one from the north brought the hide of the buffalo,
    and fine carved bones, of which he had made flutes and necklaces,
    and he wanted to trade these flutes and the necklaces and the gems that he had gathered,
    for corn and beans to take back to his people.

And the brother from the south had brought feathers,
    carrying them through the land of the Apache, to get to our village,
        and trade for corn and beans.

 Do you not see the irony?

That these brothers came home with worthless trinkets,
    to trade for the food of the village.

They met each other at the entrance to the village,
    and the one said to himself,"Aah, I see another trader,
    I will try to make good trade, and give him my beads, for something to eat."

And the other brother was thinking to himself,
    "Ah-ha, at last I will be able to trade some of these worthless feathers for food,
    for I have not eaten for days, and my people starve to the south."

And they approached each other,
    and offered what they had to trade,
        and the one brother offered ornaments, necklaces and earrings,
        and the other brother offered feathers,
            and each thought the other's objects were worthless.

And they went to the chief of the Pueblo,
    and they said, "Look what we have brought to trade for corn and beans."

And the chief looked at what they had,
    and he shook his head,
    and laughed because they thought they had the things of value,
        compared to the food.

And then the shaman of the moon came forward,
     and took one of the necklaces with its beautiful carving,
          from the bones of the buffalo,
     and he took the feathers and he held them up into the air,
          and with the magic of a shaman, when he lowered his hands,
     the feathers had been woven into the necklace,
          and it was truly a thing of beauty.

And he scoffed at them all,
     for thinking only of food as sustenance for the body,
     telling them that beauty was the food of the soul.

And the brothers started to argue with each other,
     about which had the most beautiful objects to trade.

After that, he told them that the beauty was in the difference of their objects.

He told them that the moon was of beauty, and the sun was of substance,
     and that the Great Mystery, in his wisdom had given us both,
          substance and beauty.

As a reward for bringing the gifts of beauty,
     the two brothers were given homes, one on each side of the moon.
     And now they spread their beauty every night.

Thank you. Now, let us return to the village before it is dark.

Reflecting Anger
September 17, 1998

Come.
Come with me to the pool.

Do you see in the still water an image?

Do you see the face of one who is angry and hurting?
If you can see her,
If you can see her,
> know that there is danger
> and it does not have to be.

Can you tell me more?

The danger appears to be near water.
Do you?
There is so much anger.

It is good to try to understand anger, but it is never good to feed it.

(During this particular time, medication was no longer able to control my diabetes, and I was learning to give myself shots of insulin. The grief of the initial diagnosis of diabetes resurfaced, along with frustration with my body, for not behaving normally. It now became vital to wear my medic alert necklace, which in my anger, I deemed my "defective person" tag.

Aggravating the anger was the knowledge that no matter how hard I had tried to fight my way back from near death, it wasn't enough for the church denomination I had served for my entire adult life. The bishop had informed me of her intent to remove me from the clergy roster, unless I could increase my work load by October. This was September, and hope was fading fast.

Following this talk, the Old Indian was silent for a very long time. Giving up my role within the church hurt far more than I could anticipate, and with the hurt came increased anger. Physically, depression and diabetes are a deadly duo at best, and spiritually, I was drained. It was easy to focus instead on preparing for my parents fiftieth anniversary in December. But once that celebration was over, life was difficult. Holy Week was especially rough, until Good Friday, when I heard again the voice of hope and encouragement. That episode follows.)

Share the Stories
April 2, 1999
Good Friday evening

You must look beyond, you must look beyond the circle of the flames
      when, when you cleanse.

You look through the smoke, you will see the valley
      and if you look closely, if you look with your mind, and not just your eyes,
      you will see yesterday.

 It is the folly of people, all people,
      that we seek to possess what cannot be held.

We possess our anger, we wear it like a fancy robe, or plume.

      Do not let yourself be possessed by anger.

Anger and hurt; free yourself, discard them.

Rip these emotions from your throat, and throw them into the cleansing flame.
      They hold you back.

I want to tell you a story.

First, ____ put some more wood on the fire, and make some sage tea.
Remember what I told you about the ways of the ancients?

I'm sorry, I've forgotten.

The white sage is the dispeller of negative thought.

When you drink the white sage tea, smoke the white sage tobacco,
      you free yourself to be happy,
      you permit yourself to be in harmony.

As we travel through all our cycles, as we walk in the circles of time,
      there is no time, there is no energy
      for these burdens.
            They hold us back.

When you have stories to tell, and I have stories to tell,
      I will ask you to do this;
            to bring the juniper fire, and breathe the smoke.

The juniper?

Yes.
Breathe the juniper smoke, to cleanse the mind.

Play the music, play the music of the flute,
Let it flow through your mind; let it flow through your body.

This is the old way, but it is a way that works.
It is the way to focus, when there is much to do,
      and a need to be in harmony with ourselves,
      to do the good work, to tell the stories the others need to hear.

And you do want me to be sharing the stories.

What have I done with you?
Have I not shared them with you?
      Yes, you have.

Then how could you do less, and be in harmony?

Thank you for that permission, for I will do it in a written form,
and when opportunity presents, I will tell the stories verbally,
      for that is their true nature.

But, as a writer, I was hoping you wanted the stories shared with more.

Hank and I have been talking about that lately,
      and we feel the time is right to share the stories,
      and that I am the one who heard them, so should be the one to tell them.

Hank is good,
      but he uses too many words! (he whispered, and I couldn't help but laugh!)

Is there anyone whose permission we need to ask?

      Tell the story so that the one who hears is a part of it.

Do we need to contact the Acoma Pueblo before seeking publication of the stories?

What I have shared with you
        is not Acoma;

What I have shared with you is more than Acoma,
        To be Acoma, would be to limit in time and space.

Do you see this stick that I walk with?
Uhmhm.
Do you see the carving in it?
Uhmhm.

Is this stick less a part of the juniper tree,
        because I have caressed it and carved it and polished it?
No. It is just more loved.

So it is with the stories of all peoples.

How vain to say (thumping chest) "This is MY story."
        How foolish.

The stories are like the leaves on the trees.
        The stories are like the raindrops on the lake.

Why do we tell stories?
        Think on this. This not a question to be answered quickly.
        Why do we tell stories?

The stories you have told have helped us through difficult times.

Do you think that there might be others that need to hear?

Already some people are, through the book The Family Caregiver's Journal;
        the Blanket story is in there.

What book is this?

This is Hank's book that we put together after caring for his mother,
it is a guide for helping the people who are caring for a loved one who is terminally ill.

It uses stories and poetry, as well as information, to lighten the load.

A heavy book to lighten the load!

Yes.

Interesting.

Does he tell the stories well?

He tells the story as you told the story, for I wrote it down, or I taped it, I am not sure which, when you told the story of the blanket, as Hank's mother was dying. I recorded it in some fashion, and it is word for word as you told it. It is of Napalo, who could not weave at the loom, but could weave the most beautiful stories, and of how each of us weaves a soul blanket, and when it is ready, we go to the Great Mystery.

We are all of the Great Mystery.

The Great Mystery has many faces, because the Great Mystery has many children.
	And each one of his children sees the Great Mystery with a different face.

(Whispered:) Think, think about the kiva,

Think on the kiva?

Yes, and how it was built. Do you not understand?
	The kiva is a drum. Look at how they are built.

The dancer in the drum of the kiva made the music of the Great Mystery,
	made the music of the heart of each of us.

If you will go to the valley of the ancient ones,
	stand at the sunset, and listen to the wind; it will carry the voice of the kiva.

Is that the place called Chaco Canyon, or another place of the ancient ones?

There are many places of the ancient ones.

Look also to the other ancients, look to the Ho'okum, look to the Mogollon,
	The Ho'okum and the Mogollon?

Yes.

To understand the Great Mystery, it is necessary to understand all the children.

To many of the children, the Great Mystery bring great sacrifices,

Some scoff at these,
>   but I will tell you fools lacking in understanding, scoff and disbelieve.
>   Wise are the ones who seek understanding.
>   Wise are those whose wisdom in here (pointing to his heart.)

Don't seek to just know, seek to understand,
>   and when you tell your stories, tell them with understanding.
>   Tell them with the heart.

Do you understand?

Yes, I think I do; for I know the difference between head knowledge and heart knowledge.

That is a great wisdom. A rare wisdom.

In the stories, of each of the Great Mystery's children,
>   are beautiful sights, for you see,
>   each of the people are wonderfully, beautifully different.
>   We are like flowers in the desert.
>   We are all beautifully different, but we are all still flowers.

How sad that after so many years of peace,
>   and the exchange of wisdom and possessions,
>   the ancient ones were forced to move;
>   how sad.

(While changing the tape, I missed some, and tried to recapture the essence of what he said.)

...how can we have hard times; all of the wisdom we've learned
if we battle ourselves.

You made the wise statement about peace ought to be the reality, and war the illusion, but that right now war is the reality, and peace is the illusion. I wanted that on the tape, so that I would not forget it. Is there more you can say about that, or do you have other things to say?

I have said too much.

No. It is a difficult time for the world;
if we have a way to bring a message of peace and hope, we need to do that.

My child, all people, in all times, have said that these were difficult times.

    This is not a simple pessimism; it is a sign of optimism,

    when people are always convinced that Tomorrow Can Be Better;
        that's optimism.

The reality is that each and every one of us can make today what we want in it.

And yet, that is not true.

    It Is Not True.

    Because, it is only true when we work together.

Great dwellings of the ancient ones, the Pueblos of our people,
    the great buildings of all the other cultures,
    the pyramids, the stadiums,
    the Empire State Building,
        they were all created by people working together.

If we can move mountains, build lakes,
    change the course of rivers,
        then surely, we can build Peace.

What a light load that is!

Think on this.

Poetry, Music, and Healing

(A PBS radio program called "Echos" had featured a Native American flute group known as Coyote Oldman tonight, March 18, 2000. We were recording it, and Hank had gone to bed while I worked on business and home finances. Then from our bedroom I heard Hank speak in a voice not his own, and I hurried to turn on the tape recorder. Hank's own voice tonight was weak, due to a sore throat, but the Old Indian spoke quite clearly.)

Before there were so many of us,
> long, long before we had need of books,
> we had the poetry. The poetry was the song spoken,
> and through them,
> that was the way we remembered that which was important to us.

In the song, in the chant,
> the cadence registered in our brains, and that was the root of memory.

Look even today, with our small children,
> do we not teach them the songs,
> do they not use music and song in the neighborhood of Mr. Rogers,
> and Sesame Street?

And do we not wrap all of our emotions in the musical expression?

Back, long long ago, when everybody sang,
> when everybody made their own music,
> this was the way to learn,
> this was the way that the parents gave the gift of their history
> and their knowledge to the children.

In those long ago days we had songs for everything.
> There were work songs, songs ____
> songs for birth and songs for death,
> songs to make rain, and songs to stop the flood.

And something nice about memorizing the words to songs,
> and matching those words and the mental emotions of the music.

We had a culture that didn't need books, but that was because everybody sang.

When people stopped singing, then we relied on only a few singers to sing the words.

Then we went to poetry to help us remember
        and today we have abandoned that function of poetry.

And today we don't rely on memory as much.
We have artificial memory in boxes, and on disks and tapes.
        _____, virtual files,

You had asked at what point poetry developed,
        and I think we wanted the answer, "after we learned to write."

But in truth the poetry came first.
Because the poetry gave us a second meaningful reality.
(A line here I couldn't catch--the dog was jumping off of my lap, and I lost focus.)

I hope this has answered your question.

What was that last little bit? I didn't quite understand.

What did you not understand?

*I couldn't quite hear, because I had a dog making a commotion on my lap, so I just didn't hear,
        it was not so much about not understanding.*

We were talking about the origin of poetry, *uh-hmm*
        and I said that it was the second oldest use of the written word,
        but it came before we learned to write.
        The oldest use of the written word, it seems, is unfortunately accounting.

But because within our hearts is the need for beauty,
        we _____ recorded our poetry.

Thank you.

Does that answer your question?

Yes, thank you, and welcome back.

How have you been?

(Smiling) Well.

We are in a new cycle of time,
        as one of the keepers of time measures it.

There is much to do, and many, many things to see.

Spend some time forming your questions, before you seek the answers;
        this preparation will be very important to you.

Do you know of our plans to visit the Southwest?

Where do you wish to go?

We will stay in Albuquerque;
part of the time visit the Grand Canyon,
and spend some time with my family in Arizona.

Are there sites around Albuquerque you would have us see?

There is much to see.
Stand at the top of the mountain and see tomorrow;
stand in the center of Quarai, that's an old mission, a holy place before the Spanish,
stand there, and feel the past.

Take time
        to simply walk the path,
                and watch for the little things.
The little things that you will need for your medicine bag.

Walk, walk
        the trail to Tsoodzil, what is today Mount Taylor.

Most important,
        would be to just feel
        feel with your heart where you are.
        See with your soul, not your mind.

It is far more important
        to know the beauty,
        than it is to call each piece of it by name.

(After a long pause, I coughed extensively.)

You need
> the smoke of pinion and juniper
> and the ash of sage.

Do you know how to do this much healing?

I know so little about the healing.

You take a medicine bundle,
but you must do this in the ritual form,

because it is through the ritual that you become a part of the healing.

You light the medicine bundle,
> and as it smokes, you inhale.
With the ash you will mark on your forehead and on your cheeks
> (and he demonstrated, drawing a line across his forehead, and a dot on each cheek.)

The healing comes first <u>accepting</u> rather than <u>fighting</u>
> that which is making you ill.

Then, giving yourself permission to walk on the trail beyond it.

You leave
> that with which you're caught
> that which affects your head, that which affects your heart,
>
> you leave it on the trail, like an uprooted plant left to wither and die,
> > while you go on ahead of it.

This is what healing is about.

Do you understand?

I'm trying,
it's a new way to look at things,
perhaps very helpful.

Harmony is a very complex thing to understand.
And harmony is not achieved in solitude, and neither is healing.

You do not have to walk the trail yourself;
        you do not have to make the journey yourself.

Do you understand?

Yes.

Good.

Is there anyone in particular you would like me to walk along side?
Or a place I should be, to meet?

When the time is right, you will know.

You will feel it in your heart,
and this will be your teacher.

Be patient. (Whispered, shaking an index finger at me.)

It sounds like you see me as a healer at some time.

Yes.
There could be no greater honor.

Why would one seek a greater honor?

It is the greatest honor, is what I meant to say.

To find the gift to be able to heal
whatever way that may be, body, soul, all things together...

Don't, Don't you understand?
There is no body here, soul here, (pointing in opposite directions.)
Body and soul, mind and spirit, they are together. (Hands clasped)
They must be treated together.
They must be respected together.

The secret to healing self
        is in healing others,

the secret to finding comfort for self,
        is in giving comfort to others.

The secret to finding the meaning in your life,
    is in helping others to find the meaning in theirs.

This is the plan of the Great Mystery.

We have talked long, and you have much to think about. *Definitely.*

Do not try too hard to understand everything we have talked about.
When time is right, you will find the wisdom in your heart, the answers are already there.

Thank you. You are welcome.

Thank you for your wisdom, your counsel, your presence.

I enjoy being with you.
And I with you.

If
if you need to feel my presence,
all you need to do is play the flute.

Do you understand?

A recording, or am I to play the instrument myself?

There you go---
did we not start by speaking of the need for everyone to sing their own song?

If you need the answers, you need to play your own flute.

I must go now.   *Goodnight.*

Responsibility
September 1, 2000

(He does not begin in English. He speaks as one exhausted, with barely breath to go on. His whispers are almost too quiet to be heard at first, but become more emphatic later.)

It has been a long climb; I am tired.

I must rest.

Will you play your flute while we rest, we are almost to the top.

Do you know why it is that the holy people always go to the mountains?

No.

Think on this.

The Anglos see greatness in a god who controls,
        so for them the mountain is a place from which the power emanates.

For us the mountains are holy places,
        because from each mountain we can see the beauty that goes on forever,
        also we see that for which we share responsibility.

Even when the Anglos seek responsibility, they view it as control.

I think they are very insecure about their place in the world.
I think they fear too much.

Responsibility isn't something we do for someone else or to something else.

Responsibility is inside us.

I laugh when I hear Anglos try to understand
        what we mean when we speak of holy places.

We cannot decree & proclaim "This, a Holy Place"
        as if we have the power to tell God where to be!

No, in truth, the Great Mystery has made every place holy.
Every mountain, every valley, every stream, every lake
and we are a part of that, so, we too, are holy.

There is so much that they do not understand.
And they fear so much.

Let's go the rest of the way.

As we go on our journeys,
we may feel lonely,
but we are never alone.

We always have our guides.

We often do not see them, but that does not mean they're not there.

I am old.
In some cultures, old means weakness.
And it is true, in this cycle my legs are stiff, my fingers calloused and knobby.

Sometimes my throat fails me.

But, I have the wisdom of many years.

And I know that we worry too much about that which is not our concern,
and too little about that which is our responsibility.

Look! Look out on the valley! Look at the other mountains, the hills, the sky,

It is Our responsibility to SEE the beauty

It is Our responsibility to BE the beauty.

It is NOT our responsibility to Own it, to Hide it away, to Destroy it or Control it.

(Here he chokes, or is not speaking English)...that be with these gifts of the Great Mystery.

I must sit and rest again.

Come, sit with me, and look out and see,
  see with your heart, as well as your eyes.

It is important that we see with our heart.

(Something was said, not in English, so I asked him to repeat it in English for me.)

It is important to see that which is the truth, and do it.
It is also important to see that which is beyond the stars

You have much healing to do.

For you, there are great responsibilities.

Do you understand what I am saying?

Not very well.

Think on this.

There is much for you to do.

But first you must find your heart.

This will be a long and difficult journey,
  but remember that you are never alone.

You need to sing your songs,
  you have not sung with the tune of your heart for a long time.

It's true.

Yet, the joy is there, waiting for you to set it free.

Nay-i-shu-ah.

Old Man of the Fire

October 16, 2000

(It sounded like prayer chanting in a Native American language, so I rushed into the room where he
was sleeping, and started the tape recorder. Here it was late evening, but for him it must have been
the start of a day.)

Good Morning!
Good Morning!

There's a chill in the air, is there not?
Yes, there is, for the 16th of October.

I have a question for you.

Do I come to sit by YOUR fire,
       or do you join ME at mine?

Think on this.

In a long ago time, as you would measure,
       there was a young girl,
       Leall,
       and she was lost from her people,
       and wandered in circles to find her way.

And in one of her circles, it was getting dark, and she was so tired and so hungry, so thirsty.

She sat,
       beside a juniper and she wept, and she wept,
       and the tears ran down her face, and her shirt was all wet.

And she heard the call of one of the night birds
       then she looked and through the haze of her tears, a long way off
       she thought she could see the glow of the fire.

And she stood, and with a final sob, inhaled deeply,
       and thought that she could smell the smoke.
              Now we know that the smoke is the spirit of the fire,
              and it called to her, and she followed it,

And she walked and she walked and she walked.

In the dark, she was cold, and she was hungry, she had great thirst.

Finally she was so close to the fire, that she could hear the fire talking
        in the fire language crackling and snapping as the juniper will do,
                as pinion will do.

Her heart called to her to run to the fire and be warm,
        but her mind said, "Stop. And learn first whose fire this was."

So cautiously she crept up the side of the hill from the fire,
        and looked down, and there by the fire was a very old man,

And it looked like he was putting something on a stick by the fire.

She thought to herself, "This is a stranger who is a friend.
        He is cooking a meal; perhaps he will share with me."

And she walked down to the fire,
        and when she got there, there was no one there!

The warmth of the fire wrapped her with the smell of the smoke,
        was joined by the scent of the buffalo gourd root that was roasting by the fire.
And she saw at the side was a gourd of water,
        and the clay vessel with seeds.

Very softly, she called out,
        "Old Man, Old Man of the fire!
                Will you share with me?"

But there was no answer.

She called again,
        "Old Man, Old Man of the fire!
                Will you share with me?
                Will you share the warmth of your fire?
                Will you share a sip of your water?
                Will you share a bite of your food,
                For I am tired, and cold, and thirsty and hungry."

And there was no answer.

She stood closer, felt the warmth wrap around her again, and spoke one more time:
"Old Man, Old Man of the fire,
I will share the warmth, the water, and the food,
and I will thank you."

She stepped closer, and drank of the water,
and it was good, and it was fresh,
and as she sat it down, she saw that there was a blanket there.

She took the gourd root from by the fire, and with a stick cut it open,
and it was good.

And she looked into the fire,
and she thought she could see the face of an old man,
and she said, "Old Man, Old Man of the fire, I thank you."

And all she heard was the sizzle of the snap and the crackle of the flames.

And the call of the night bird in the distance.

She ate more, and with her finger carefully pulled some seeds from the cache pot.
And ate them, and ate more of the root, and drank more of the water.

Then, she thought to wrap herself in the blanket and sleep,
but she saw that the flames were not crackling as loud, or dancing as high.

She gathered more branches and added them to the fire,
and it spoke with great joy, as its flames danced again.

Then, she wrapped herself in the blanket, and lay down to sleep.

She looked one more time at the fire,
and said, "Old Man, Old Man of the flames,
you have given me so much, that I thank you for it.
I have one more question.
Which way is home?"

And she waited and she waited,
and way off in the distance,
she heard the call of the night bird again,
and she slept.

When she awoke in the morning, the flames were but warm coals, covered in their ash.
     She ate the last of the buffalo gourd root, drank some more of the water,
          and ate some more of the seeds.

With that, she began to walk in the direction of the night bird's call.

And she found her way home.

And there was great, great joy in the village,
     And that night, everyone built a great fire in the plaza,
     and they baked bread, and they had a feast,
     and they danced, and they played the flute and the drum, and they sang,
     and there was great joy.

And as she sat and gazed into the flames,
     she thought that again, for one brief moment,
          she could see an old man's face in the flames,
               And then it was gone in a wisp of smoke.

And again she heard the night bird's call, and she was happy, and comforted.

What do you think of Leall's story? *What is her name?* LEALL.

You have not answered my question.

> *I thought you might answer it.*
> *It is not good to wander alone, looking for the place one belongs.*
> *I am glad she found her way back.*

But, would she have known she was home, if she had not wandered?

Possibly, but possibly not.

You have not answered my first question.
Do I come to visit your fire, or do you come to mine?

I think you come to visit my fire, some of the time.

Why did Leall weep?
Think on this.

Was it fear, was it loneliness, was it desolation, or was it being lost?

I think it was being lost.

But, you cannot find your way, unless first you have lost it!
Is this not the essence of youth?

How did she find her way?
She did not do it alone. But she...go ahead...

You see, she never was alone.

Where does one look today for guidance?

The guidance is always there.

The Anglos make much of their books,
      there is much wisdom, much guidance in their books,
      but only if you open the book!

Within each of us
      is much wisdom...we have our own guidance.
      It is within our hearts; we need to open our hearts, and know what is there.

We need to listen to our spirit guides
and know that the great Mystery has sent them to be with us so we are never alone.

What is fire?

Energy and light, heat

Yes! Light, light and heat!

In a long, long ago time,
    we did not know fire.
    We wandered aimlessly, fearful.

Then, then the Great Mystery gave us the gift of fire.
    And we became people.

It is an instinct within us, to have Fire!

    We have the campfire, and find great comfort there.
    We light candles, we light torches,
        so that we can watch the dance of light,
        and we can be one with the light.

(The rest of this is said with a smile on his face, pointing at me often for emphasis.)

You have great wisdom.

Use it wisely.

You...are a candle.

You...are a torch.

You...are the light, the warmth and the comfort of a campfire.

Enjoy your brightness!

Sharing Gifts
November 9, 2000

(Hank seemed particularly exhausted tonight, as well he might, with all of the work he has been doing lately. Besides providing horticulture therapy sessions for eleven groups of people, he had recently been contacted about setting up some special gardens near orphanages in some third world nations. The opportunity is amazing, and we are watching how it unfolds, with much of the research being done in our own back yard. Using a micro-intensive growing system with continuous harvest and/or multi-purpose plants, the potential to help battle starvation is incredible. In the last two weeks we had books printed detailing projects for both horticultural therapy and the Abundant Harvest Gardening System. We are both tired, but thrilled.

He had gone to bed relatively early, and in his sleep had come out to the living room to sit in his recliner near me. He was making some sleep talk noises, and so I encouraged him to go back to bed, thinking to be near the tape recorder if our friend was about to visit. Evidently the Old Indian considered that an invitation! And the tape recorder didn't work, so I found myself taking dictation, much as I had during his earliest visits.)

First there was the old friend's voice speaking in a low and distant chant, a voice speaking in a different language, then the voice became stronger and was in English.

You have asked me to visit you.

It is kind of you
        to have this fire
                for warmth and light.

What is it you wanted of me?

You called for me--
        What is it you want?
        What is it you need?

(Because sometimes in the past he has begun by saying I had asked a question, and here was his answer, I waited to see if that would happen again; whether he would provide the answer as to why I had "called." This was new; he often came when we needed, but never in direct response to my "calling" of him. It soon became obvious he meant to wait for my response, so I spoke.)

I wasn't aware that I had called, but perhaps you heard my concern for Hank's health. I fear that he is pushing himself too hard, and may become seriously ill.

I know this one!
>Do not worry.
>He has much to do.

If you wish to help him, remind him to use his gifts.

Once in a long long time ago, in another cycle of time,
>the Great Mystery was in a good mood, and gave great gifts to everyone.

He gave things of beauty,
>and he gave tools to make life easier.

It is a curious thing about gifts;
>that for some, what is beautiful is thought useless.

And what is useful is thought to only be more work.

There was among those that the Great Mystery gave gifts,
>an Old Man who had a broad smile,
>>which was the gift he gave to all those who came to him.

The Great Mystery gave this man a bowl of fine clay
>and told him that this was to hold his corn.
And the Old Man smiled his smile and said,
>"Thank you. This is a fine gift."

And he took his black paint and his red paint
>and he drew the circle on the inside of the bowl
>>to symbolize life as always without beginning and without end.

And then he took his finger in the black paint,
>and he made a picture of rabbit and coyote and snake and owl and quail and deer.

Then in the middle of the bowl he made the symbols for clouds and the sun,
>because the sun is in the center of everything we do;
>because the sun is in the center of everything we ARE.

He looked at the bowl that had been a gift to him,
>and he saw what he had done with it, and he was pleased.
He smiled a great smile, for he had made beauty.

And he filled the bowl with corn,
>> and he was going to go to the center of the village
>> and show everyone his beautiful bowl.

He passed a little old lady, who looked so hungry.

He stopped, looked at her and said,
>> "Old Woman, would you like some corn?"

He smiled. She felt his face, his smile,
>> and she gave him one and said,
>>> "Thank you, thank you Old Man.
>>> I am hungry, and too old to go into the field."

He said, "Old Woman, let me give you this bowl, and the corn in it."

She said, "Thank you." And they were both happy; and he went on.

She ate the corn and it was good.

She ate for several weeks from the bowl,
>> first from around the outer edge, and revealed the red circle of life.

Then each day when she ate more,
>> another one of his drawings was revealed.

She saw the rabbit,
>> and understood that the Great Mystery gives everyone the gift of speed and motion,
>> and she gave thanks to the Great Mystery.
She saw the owl,
>> and understood that the Great Mystery gives everyone the gift of wisdom,
>> and again she gave thanks.
As she ate the corn, she found each animal the old man had painted,
>> and uncovered more gifts the Great Mystery gives to everyone.

And she gave thanks to the Great Mystery for each gift,
>> until finally one day the bowl was empty.

She took her juniper twigs and her sage,
>> and she put them in the bowl,
>> and she walked out in to the fields.

Then she gathered her herbs in the bowl,
       and she thought that she would take them into the village to trade for more corn.

But along the way, she saw a Mother, with a Child who was ill.
       She took the bowl to the Mother and said,
       "Here, this is a gift that will make your child well."
       And she taught the Mother to make the teas, and burn the sage and juniper.
       And then she walked on,

And the Child was made better!

He and his Mother took the bowl and went to the cornfield,
       and filled the bowl with corn pollen,
       and they went to the village.

Mother said, "We will build a great fire;
       all the drummer and flute players will be there,
       and everyone will be there to sing and dance
              because the Child is well,
              and we have corn pollen to give to the Great Mystery.

And they built the fire,
       and everyone came to the fire.

But the Child said,
       "Where is the Old Woman who gave us the bowl with the herbs?"

One of the drummers said, "I know who it is that you speak of."
       And he found her and brought her, and she was pleased.

She said, "But where is the Old Man who brought me the bowl of corn?"

And a flute player said, "I know who it is that you speak of."
       And he went and brought the Old Man.

And the Old Man was pleased, and he smiled,
       and he gave smiles to everyone,
       and he clapped his hands with the music.

The Child came to him with the bowl of corn pollen and said,
       "Old Man, will you take a pinch of pollen as a gift to the Great Mystery?"
       And the Child gave each person a pinch of pollen
              to throw to the East to say Thank You.

In the bowl was one pinch of pollen left,
        and the Child smiled, and gave the gift of his smile to the Old Man,
        and gave the Old Man the bowl, and said,
        "I brought it full of pollen, and now it is full of smiles."

And as the Old Man took the last of the pollen,
        where he had painted the sun in the center of the bowl,
        it reflected the bright light of the fire.

It was the smile of the Great Mystery.

We are all given gifts;
        it is what we do with them that is important.

It is not important to HAVE the gift;
It is important, to GIVE the gift.

The Old Man could have kept the bowl,
        but what would have happened to the Old Woman?

She could have kept the bowl,
        but what would have happened to the Mother and Child?

The Child could have kept the bowl,
        and the village would not have seen the smile of the Great Mystery.

You, too, have many gifts. (Pointing a finger at me.)

You have asked me about Hank.
        He has gifts,
        and like the Old Man, he is trying to give them to others.

This is good.

Do not worry about him.

I think the Great Mystery smiles
　　　　but you have other questions you wanted to ask me---

I'm not even sure what the questions would be;
　　　　perhaps I seek help to find my place, for you see things more clearly.

When you see the brightness of the sun (demonstrating with his hand, fingers extended)
　　　　and the cloud passes in front of it (which he shows with the other hand)
　　　　is not the sun still there?

Tell me, which will be there tomorrow?

I hear that rain is predicted, but it will pass, and the sun will shine.

The sun will be there tomorrow;
　　　　the light is always there,
　　　　　　　　in the sun,
　　　　　　　　in your heart. (Pointing to his own chest.)

I understand the importance of sharing one's gifts, but I no longer know how to do that,
　　　　plus make a living, provide insurance, and so on.

You worry,
　　　　and what is to be done you will know.

But first you must accept your gifts;
　　　　you cannot share them, until you accept your gifts.

Can you be of any help to identify them for me?

The Anglos would say you have been much blessed with two beauties.
　　　　(Indicating this with 2 fingers waving and pointing at me.)
　　　　You have a beautiful face, like the flower, you have great beauty.
　　　　But you also have a beautiful mind.

These are two of your gifts.

But you have another, another that is so rare.

      You have a beautiful heart.

You have much to do, and many people that need you.

It is interesting. I think that you want to tell me "What is tomorrow?"
      As if all of time was a book we read one page a day.
          But tomorrow isn't written yet!!!

I can tell you much of the future:
I can tell that tomorrow morning, the sun will rise;
      that winter will come, and the mountain tops will be covered with snow.

I can tell you that tomorrow the rivers will flow,
      and that there will be waves upon the ocean.

I can tell you that in the future, apple trees will be in blossom,
      and in another future, the blossoms will become fruit.

What more do you need to know?

Who is it that needs me, for sometimes I feel so worthless.

NO. NO. NO.
The Great Mystery would not give these gifts, and then have you be worthless.

You need a different word.
      You are PRICELESS.

Do you remember the story I told you a long time ago,
      of the hunter who went looking for the deer?

Yes, I do, of how the deer was the Great Mystery, who provided for the village when the hunter spared his life, and they did the deer dance in his honor, because he had fed the village.

You have learned well!

Think again on gifts.

You need to share your gifts.

You need to understand, that YOU ARE A GIFT.

Then may the Great Mystery open the doors for me to see a direction, and follow.

When it is time, you will know it here; (indicating his head.)
When it is time, you will know it here. (Indicating his heart.)

For now, you need to weed your garden.

I'm sorry, I don't recall what you mean by that.

First, in your mind,

      weed out fear (tossing it one way)

      weed out doubt (tossing it another way.)

         They're great weeds.

Be Patient

December 18, 2000

(We had been having a discussion about faith, and where Jesus Christ fit in with our individual experience of church and spirituality. I am a Christian by birth and faith, and yet have worshiped along side of Jewish neighbors and Spiritualist friends, and find great comfort in the wisdom of a certain Indian Storyteller. Tonight I was wrestling with the importance of keeping my observance of Christmas focused on the birth of God With Us, Emmanuel.

Yet at the same time my heart resists the concept of God demanding the sacrifice of Jesus' life to atone for our sins. I have no problem with the Resurrection, having had profound spiritual experiences in my own life, that open me to the great possibilities of God's power. I have no problem with the inclusiveness of Christ's love, a radical concept for that time. But I do question the vicarious suffering of Jesus, taking on the punishment for the sins of the world. Could, would, a gracious God expect or demand that?

Hank is called to help feed the hungry, and may have to have other employment for awhile, in order to fulfill his longing to provide direct care. This is incredibly difficult to comprehend for him, when he knows that daily children are starving, and he has information and a system that could help provide the nourishment to sustain their lives. Yet something within me said, "Slow down," when he proposed founding a nonprofit organization. And at the Spiritualist church we visited, he was given the same message from one of his grandfathers. He is exhausted, and I have encouraged him to take time to listen, perhaps in a retreat. I think it is hard for him to hear anything but the cries of starving children right now; but when our Storyteller friend spoke up tonight, his message was also one about slowing down. It is still strange to hear words coming from Hank physically, but bringing a message that I am supposed to tell him. He will hear them in the voice not his own, when he listens to the tape of the conversation that follows.)

Could you speak a little louder? I can't quite hear you.

Welcome.

Thank you.

Thank you for sharing the_____ with me.

You thanked me for something? Sharing the beauty.

Look, down in the valley--
    the snow--so beautiful, is it not?

Yes, it is.

It is truly a special time of the year.
You have questions.

Let us walk while we talk.

What is it you wish to ask me?

I know that Hank has been given the gift of passion to feed the hungry...
This is good!

This is very good.
I know him well. He has a good heart.
Yes, he does.
But he has little patience....

This is the time of the year
      when we gather juniper branches
      and tie bells on our ankles,
      and we will dance the winter dance.

It is sad; your people do not dance.
      I am told that in some of the churches,
      they do not allow dancing. How strange.
          Why is it?

It might arouse passion.

And that is bad??? (We both chuckled.)
In the eyes of some, yes, it is.

Should we not feel strongly about the Great Mystery,
      when we dance the Dance of Thanks?
Uh-hum.

I know the Anglos observe this season with much passion.
They prepare great feasts, decorate much, and give many gifts.

But you have questions.

I don't even know what to ask.

As we go through our cycles, we gain experience and wisdom.

Before your people came,
        we did not know about the baby, born among the sheep.
           We didn't even know about sheep!

And then the Spanish came,
        at first they told us about the crosses,
        and we were confused.

But then, they told us about the baby (He whispered)
        in a far, far distant tribe.

We were wise and learned much of their faith.

Think on this.
(Gesturing with his right hand.)
We had our faith. We knew the Great Mystery our way,
        and that faith was in one hand.

And then, (gesturing with his left hand)
        we learned about Jesu--
        and that faith was in our left hand.

See how rich we are?

Two faiths, one Great Mystery.
Life is simple. (He whispered, so I had to ask *What is simple?*)
LIFE is simple.

This is the time of the year
        when we look for the great beauty inside us all.

And it is there.

You need to tell Hank
        to be patient.

You also need to be patient.

When we stand in the forest
        surrounded by the trees
        we can't see the beauty of the forest.

When we climb the mountain
       we are closer to the sky
       and above the forest.

You Need--to get above the forest.
You Need--to get above the trees.

So does this one you call Hank.

You need--your mountain.

I have told you before of sacred mountains,
       of holy places, and I told you that all places are holy.

(He's breathless.)
Stop. I must sit and rest.

Please, catch your breath.

You one time wrote a story.

I want you to read that story today.

You are wiser now than you were when you wrote it.

Are you talking about <u>Ponder the Mystery,</u> or another story?

It is your Christmas story. *That would be it.*

This is important to you.
       Read it again. *I will.*
       There is something in it for you.

I want you to....(he is worn out.)

What do you want me to do?

There is much good in your heart.
Use your good well.

Watch the trail.

I must go now. *Thank you.*

The Wisdom of the Red Corn People
October 8, 2001

(Words spoken softly, with the gestures that accompany the start of a visit from our friend.)

It is time to celebrate the harvest seasons.

(Another tongue seems to be spoken.)

I am having difficulty hearing you. Could you speak just a little louder please? I know that it is time to celebrate the harvest season, but I couldn't hear after that.

Do you know of the Red Corn People?

No, could you tell me about them, please?

Again words in another language I could not understand, before he told the following story.

In those days,
the corn was planted,
and as it grew, they would pull the soil up around each stalk.

Datalel fell, and after that, could not run.

But by walking slow, living one step at a time,
    he saw things;
    he saw the way the blades of grass laid on top of each other in patterns,
        and he wove baskets in these patterns.

He saw the tiny colored stones,
    and pressed them into the moist clay of the pots and jars.

One time Datalel was walking slowly and could not keep up with the others because of his limp,
and he saw a corn stalk, that was growing bigger than all of the others around it.

And he stopped to look at it.

And he noticed that instead of having the soil pulled up in a little hill around it,
    it had been neglected, and had a little hole , and when it rained, the water stayed,
    and this puddle fed the stalk, and let the corn plant drink all it wanted, so it grew bigger.

And he went back to his corn field,
    and built little holes of dirt around each stalk, and everyone laughed at him.

They laughed at him in the time of knee corn.
But when the harvest came, no one laughed.

For the ears on his corn were the biggest by far.
And in the joyful time of harvest, his family had more corn than all the others.

And he took the seed of the biggest ears,
        it was red; the corn was in many colors,
        and that is why some are called the yellow corn people,
        and some are called the blue corn people.

Datalel's people were ever after called the Red Corn Clan.

And the South People would come carrying their feathers.
And the North People would come carrying buffalo hides.
And the Big Water People would come carrying shells.
All to trade for the red corn.

Datalel would sit and smoke the pipe, and weave the baskets as the grass had taught him,
and he would trade bright feathers for rugs and the shells.

For these people were Planter People.

And they trade with all who come.

In those days,
        there were people who did not plant.

They would raid, and steal, that which they could not grow.

Datalel would tell the story, that no one raids in the time of knee corn.

They raid always in time of harvest.

When the Big Water People traded the shells,
Datelel and the Red Corn Clan would take the shells, drill holes in them,
        and weave them together for their ankles for the dance.

For it is a truth, (shaking his finger for emphasis)

that for all people, the joy of the dance cannot be denied.

Datalel, even lame, would strap on the shells to his ankles and wrists, and he would dance.

The drum and the flute made the music,
        and each of the dancers was also making music.
                This, this is one of the great gifts of the Great Mystery.

When the people who did not know how to plant came to raid,
the Red Corn People, the Red Corn People were in the field harvesting.

And they rose up and surrounded the others.
And they said, "Why do you raid our field?
        Come, come dance with us, and celebrate the harvest."

And the other people were ashamed,
        and they said, "We will be back in two days," and they departed.

And in the evening of the second day,
        they came to the People of the Red Corn,
        bringing deer and turkey,
        and together they had a feast,
        and they learned to dance the harvest dance.

And Datelal taught them how to plant the corn,
        and how to read the signs of the moon,
        and he gave them seed pots filled with his best corn.
        And they went away.

In the spring that followed, they planted their corn,
        and it grew up.

And in the fall, when the time of the harvest,
        they came to the Red Corn People and said,
        "Come with us, and bring your squash and beans,
        for we wish to share our corn with you."

And that is the way harvest dance came to the others, and they raided no more.

(Pointing at me, with an approving tone and smile:)
You grow good words.

In the harvest season, share them.

You grow words that comfort. Share them.

Ishneah,
Dance in the cool evening, by the light of the fire.

vashishneah,

When I was old, I could no longer dance.
Dance when you can; sing when you can.

Do you know of the corn pollen? Have we spoken of this?

That to use it to greet the morning with respect? Or do you have other meanings in mind?

It is not to greet the morning, as much as it is to greet the Great Mystery.
And thank the Great Mystery for the gift of morning, for the gift of the sun.

Do you know why we use corn pollen?
No, I don't.

Think on this.

The corn is the physical body,
as you are the physical body.

The pollen is the spirit of the corn that is released into the air and floats.
Without the pollen, the ear of corn can never be complete, and the corn plant is never fulfilled.

As it is with you, without the spirit, and physical you are never complete, and not fulfilled.

The pollen is the spirit of the growing plant,
        and that is why we offer it with this gift, this recognition of the Great Mystery.

It is important to speak to the Great Mystery as a friend.
It is important to thank the Great Mystery as a friend.

That is why we toss the pinch of corn into the dawn. (The what?) The DAWN.
That is why we look to the east and the rising sun.

And we say thank you
for our people are Planters.

Do you understand? Hishneyah, atuate,

Seek the wisdom of the Red Corn People.

Ishotowa. Hicontua. Ishco. Oshomato-ye. *Thank you.*

(We received this story just when our country was bombing Afghanistan, in retaliation for the destruction of the World Trade Center and damage to the Pentagon. In our hearts we know it is better to feed your enemies, and make them your friends, than to destroy them through the use of force. So it is with deep sadness we hear of our own damage to a people so downtrodden already, even if we know the world demands "justice" to be done.)

Totems and Spirit Guides
The Quest for the Green Parrot
March 16, 2002

(He starts gesturing with his right hand, the left arm positioned so that his elbow is directly over his face. The first sounds are not English, but I couldn't hear well enough to write it as it sounds. Then I greeted him, and the conversation began.)

Hello.
Eye-ishitay

The fog is thick today;
I cannot see the next step.

I am right here, beside you.

You are telling stories? That we have shared?
Have, have you told of the green parrot?

No, but I have been very curious. Friends were mentioning the green parrot just this week.
The kachina of the green parrot.

You would know that in the days of the ancient ones
        and even before

the bird was good medicine.

The parrot? What kind of bird--what was the good medicine, I missed it.

The parrot. *Ok, thank you.*

In the land of the sacred mountains, parrots flew in those days
        yet today, they are there no more.

In those days, the parrot would care for the men and women of the village
        and the parrot was the totem of many women.

There was much power and wisdom in that bird.
And it was as they were caring for the parrot, the women gained strong counsel.

And the villages,
in the days even before the days of the villages,
the people raised the parrots,
not because they were strong (made a fist.)
Not because they were good to eat. Parrot is not good to eat!

But because the parrot brought on its wings the gift of beauty.

The green parrots were like the magpies today.
They would stay with the people, visit them at their fires.

And bring messages from far away.

You are going far away, are you not?

Yes. Very soon,

You will make good counsel.

Thank you. I will try.

You are good medicine, you know.
Because you have the heart of a wise leader.

You have great strength there (pointing to my heart.) You need not fear.

But you do need to tell the stories.

Do you know the traditions of telling stories?
All over, in all of the tribes. It is the stories of each tribe that makes us all one people.

These stories you must tell. You must also paint the pictures.
In, in your heart, and in your mind, you have the pictures that tell the stories.

You also have the gift of kind words.

You, you must use the gift.
You must also seek as your quest the green parrot,
and know that in those wings
is your spirit guide.
Really...

Understand that in different times we have different needs,
>   so the Great Mystery sends us different guides.
>   And we don't have just one. Do you know your totems?

I used to...I don't recall them so well right now.

Think. *The white buffalo?* Why white?

I don't know. Perhaps that is how it appeared to me in a dream.

Once, long long ago, when your spirit was young, you were of the Buffalo Clan.
And it didn't have to be white.
No.

Would another totem be the bird that has come to look in the kitchen window?
Several birds, actually, the hummingbird, and the hawk?

The hummingbird, and the hawk are two, two powerful totems. Both are messengers of the
Great Spirit. Both hear prayers.
You, you need to watch the ways of the hummingbird. There are stories there for you to tell.
Uh-hmm.
In many places it is thought that if the story is not old, it has been told many, many times,
it is not a good story. But this was not the way of the tellers tradition.

The story can be told and retold and told in many ways.
This is an ORAL TRADITION the anthropologist says. *Uhhmm*
(Almost angry as he says this.) It is Not a pictoglyph etched in stone!

The story is a living thing that grows and changes as it answers the needs of different people.
And the same story can be heard by different people to mean many different things.
There is wisdom in your heart. *That was the old preacher talking. I never knew when I told a*
story from the pulpit, what would be heard. I could only give it my best intentions.
What more does the Great Mystery ask? *Not much, I guess.* No.

Could you tell me more about my totems?
If that's important?

It is important to know two things;
totems are guide posts; totems show you the way of your heart.
They show you what is in your soul.
Totems are with you; they are not spirit guides.
Spirit guides are there when you need them. And they change.

We, we can think of spirit guides as angels in some cultures.
But, the Great Mystery is wise, to reveal to us only what we can handle at this time.
Trust the Great Mystery and know that we are all a part of the Great Mystery.
Neither totems or spirit guides are the spirits of ancestors.

There is much we don't know, much we can't know.

Your totems are with you forever. Your spirit guides change as your needs change.
Your husband Hank one time had as a spirit guide, a coyote.
He also at one time had an ape. *Ah-ha!* As a spirit guide.
Watch with him as a new spirit guide is revealed to him.
And this will be important to both of you, because the new spirit guide will also be yours.

It is important to know that you and your husband are of one heart.
You are both of the Gentle People.

It is time now for you to ask us some questions.

If the totems are with me forever, could you remind me who they are,
        and what they mean, how they work with me,
        how I can work with them, or play with them?

(He smiles.) Wise words.
The buffalo is the most ancient of your totems.
        It is the totem of nurturing and provision.
        Remember in the wisdom of the buffalo it is the wise cow who leads.

(Laughter) Why do you laugh?
I come from a tradition that is just beginning to accept the leadership of women.
        It sounds as if the buffalo have been ahead of us on this.
You need to seek as your quest the story of the green parrot; there is great wisdom there for you.
Good.
The hummingbird is another of your totems.
Beauty, swiftness, there are many stories of the hummingbird, and how it would carry the
messages to the Great Mystery, and bring answers back.
I remember you talking of the hummingbird as that messenger, when Hank's mother was very ill.
The hummingbird also was a messenger, but the hawk is not your totem. *Ok.*
The hawk is a spirit guide.
Watch the hawk.
Another totem of yours, another powerful medicine, is the cat. *Hmmm.*
Think on this.

The Great Mystery sometimes gives us the great gift of a totem we can see and touch and feel.

Sometimes the totem is from a different time and a different place and a different cycle.
The totem is always with you. You always belong to that totem.

You will do much travel this year.
And you will discover much. You are kind of heart, and give your husband a great gift.
But the journey you make is a gift to you also.
You will be going HOME.
You will make great discoveries.
You and Hank will find a new spirit guide this year. Watch, listen, feel!

It is important, very important
        for you to give counsel on peace, guide Hank in this.
        Your wisdom is greater, and your spirit wiser.

You have another question.
Yes, I do. What do you mean by I will be going home?

You will be in the place you have been before,
        and when you are there, you will know it, you will feel it in your heart,
        you will be drawn back to this place.
I think you may have been there before.

Any clues? What state it is in, since we have many travels planned?
States. *Arbitrary, I am sure.* No. Your mountain. *Mount Taylor?* (He smiles.)
I told you, you had great wisdom.
It is a place of great joy.
That is a powerful place. You have talked with one who knows much, and yet is one of your
faith. His mind is limited. Do not be afraid to be a shining light. Do not be afraid to give counsel
and new ideas. This is what progress is. Otherwise, we become slaves to yesterday.

You have another question.
I just seem to have so much to learn. Good. (Smiles) but you also have learned much.

This one you speak of that knows much but has a limited mind, with a faith we share,
I am wondering who that is; I don't know if it matters or not.
I did not say you shared a faith. You both have a faith.
You spoke with him in a holy place. *Ok. Mr. Elmer Leon, from the Santa Ana Pueblo.*
(Smiling) A wise man; *Uh-hmm. Will we meet him again?* Perhaps.
You will meet many others. You will meet many who are seeking.
Many who are on a quest, without a goal.

The work we are doing with the gardens, is this something that will truly be beneficial to many,
as we dream it might be?

114

Your dreams are good and powerful, and your dreams, are from the heart.
Many people, many people all over will thank you. Yes, when you care enough to work this hard,
when you follow the request that you feed the hungry, clothe the naked, love your neighbor
when you live in your heart this way, it is powerful medicine.
These again are stories to tell.

I was thinking about something you said about the cat being my totem...
Is that why Scooter could tell us of Hank's mother's difficulties,
Toby could tell me it was time to get up and go be with my parents, they needed us that day,
Tucker has been there constantly with me through pain and sorrow and joy,
Katie, Hank's mother talked about watching the angels with her. Are all cats connected to me,
or just the ones I have brought into my home? I am still waiting..Sassy is still young.

You do not understand the power of totem.
No, I really don't. Anything you could tell me would help.

All life is spirit. All of life is connected. Some call it energy.
Some call it other things.

There are, there are forces that you can not yet understand.
But were once understood by all peoples.
Know this, each animal in a species is a part of over all spirit, is connected to the Great Mystery.
That does not mean that each of those is connected personally to you.
Your white cat *Tucker* is special, connected to you.
The one you called Scooter *yes* was sent for a purpose.
The one you call Toby has a purpose.
Other cats may have other purposes; it is vain to think that all life is here to serve you;
but it is just the opposite. Think on this.
To have a totem not only means that you receive,
it means you are expected to give.

We have talked long, *yes*, I am tired.
I am thankful for the conversation, and know I will be learning from it for a long time.

Can I help you in any way?

You have. It is important to tell the stories. This is one of your talents.
Weave the good story.
Be cautious of those who profess great knowledge.
(Whispered.)I thank you for spending time with me. *Thank you as well.*

Coyote and the Feather

May 8, 2002

(On a trip to North Dakota, I had found and purchased a figurine of a coyote seated on a bench, wrapped in a blanket, wearing a hat that had one feather in the hatband. Hank had mentioned that someday he'd have to write a story about that coyote. Then one night after he had gone to sleep, he came back to the study where I was working, sat down on one of the chairs, and proceeded to tell this entire tale. I took dictation as he spoke and gestured. He had no memory of it the next morning, and wondered how it had gotten on the computer, if he could have written it, so I explained that he told it while I typed. It is actually more powerful when told than read, as are many of the stories from the Old Indian. It was not told in our friend's voice, as this storyteller spoke much faster and used more repetition as an effective tool in the telling. But I have chosen to include it just the same, as it came to us mysteriously, and gives us something to ponder.)

Coyote was a curious and envious fellow.
He watched the hummingbird, and thought,
> "Oh, how I long to fly like a hummingbird, swift and beautiful I would fly;
> fast, fast I would fly." But he could not fly.

Coyote watched the magpies as they moved along the desert, and then up, up to the treetops,
and he thought,
> "Oh, how I wish I could fly like the magpie, up, up to the treetops.
> I could see things and then talk to the other birds about all I saw.
> How I wish I could fly like a magpie."

Then Coyote saw an eagle, soaring, soaring high over head.
And he said,
> "Oh, how I wish I could fly like an eagle, and soar, soar so high in the sky.
> Think of all I could see, if only I could soar so high like the eagle."
> But of course, he could not fly.

Then Coyote encountered the Great Mystery,
and told the Great Mystery of the birds he had observed.

And the Great Mystery told him, "Of course the birds can fly, for they have the gift of feathers."

And Coyote responded,
> "Yes, they do, but I am wise, and if I only had *one* feather, I am certain I could fly.

So the Great Mystery told him that yes, it would be so,
> that Coyote should watch for a special feather,
> one that would allow him to fly for just one day.

116

And Coyote was happy. He went on his way, and soon he found a beautiful big blue feather.
 "This is it!" He proclaimed.
 "This is my special feather, my gift from the Great Mystery."

But Coyote was aware that it was almost noon,
 and if he were to use the feather today, it would only be good for part of the day.
 So he tucked it in his hat, planning to save it for the next day.

As he walked along,
he met Rabbit, and Bear, and Turtle, and Owl, and Armadillo and other friends.
He showed them his feather and said,
 "Look, with this feather, tomorrow I too can fly!"
But all of the other animals shrugged their shoulders.
They could not understand why Coyote would even want to fly.

It became evening, and Coyote was cold,
so he wrapped his blanket close around him, and went to sleep.
The Great Mystery sent Brother Wind to play a trick on the trickster,
 which Wind thought to be great fun.
It blew Coyote's beautiful big blue feather far, far away.

When he awoke, Coyote's feather was gone!
He went to find the Great Mystery and complained that it had disappeared in the night,
 and had not even been used yet.
Great Mystery smiled and said,
 "You have tried to hoard the gift, and now it has blown far, far away.
 When you find it, and you will, you are to use the gift immediately."

Coyote looked everywhere.
He looked in the valley, along the arroyo.
He looked on top of the mesa.
He even climbed the tall mountain, and there, there it was!
On the very top of the high mountain was his beautiful big blue feather.

Coyote grabbed the feather, and this time did not hesitate.
He immediately began to fly, fly fast and darting, fast as the hummingbird;
fly high, high as the tree tops, just like the magpies.
Coyote even soared farther and farther from earth,
 looking down on it from up where only eagles go.

And flying was everything he had hoped it would be,
 and he enjoyed this gift from the Great Mystery.

Bear and Rabbit and Turtle and all of the others watched,
but could not understand why Coyote wanted to fly, so they went about their own business.

Coyote did not notice that night was fast approaching, and he had traveled far.
He landed and discovered that he knew not where he was.
He had flown too fast and too far, without taking any notice of which way would take him home.

Isn't there a bit of Coyote in each one of us?

Green Apple Stew

June 2002

I-ish-ne-ah

(*I-ish-ne-ah*)

na-sta-ha-deh-seh

Hello.

(More I couldn't understand.)

It is a nice evening, is it not. *It is.*

The fire is reflected in the stars.

Thank you for inviting me.

You have questions?

You are going on a trip soon. *Yes.*
What will you be seeing?

We are going to the Albuquerque area, and may look at property,
*   are considering moving out there, but don't know as of yet,*
*   how we would make a living, that sort of thing, but feel pulled in that direction.*

You smile.

This is a strange term that you use, to Make A Living.
How does one do that?

Find enough money to meet the bills, by working or whatever means it takes,
*   to find employment or create a job,*
*   services for which payment will be exchanged for other goods needed for life.*

I see.
When you are there, go to the Salt Valley; there is something you need to learn there.
Then after the Salt Valley, go to the Mountain Where the Sun Sets. It is good medicine.

Would that be Mount Taylor?
That is what you call it.

Do you know of the green apple stew? *No, I really don't.*

It is a story. I will tell you.

That one time, the People and all of the Animal People talked with each other.
And one day, there was much hunger,
        and Crane and Hummingbird went to the Wise Man who lived in the Rainbow Cave.

It was up to Crane and Hummingbird because only the People Who Could Fly could get to this cave, steep in the cliffs.

The wise elder who lived there greeted them.
And they said all the people were hungry.

And he gave them a bowl,
        and told them to fly in each direction, North, South, East, and West.
        And gather honey and green apples.

So, they took the bowl back to the village,
Then set out,
        the crane flapping his great wings, soared into the sky,
        and that evening returned with one green apple,

and the hummingbird, who back in those days was only white,
        darted from here to there, from flower to flower, and followed honeybee to her hive.
        And asked the bee if she might have a sip of the honey.

And she brought a little honey back, and put it in the bowl.

And in the morning, the crane flapped his great white wings, and went north,

And Hummingbird darted from flower to flower,
        and followed another honeybee, this time to the north,
And that evening Crane brought back one green apple,
        and Hummingbird, one sip of honey.

The next day, Crane flapped his great white wings again,
        and went to the south.
And Hummingbird darted here and there, and followed a honeybee to her hive again,
        and that evening Crane returned with one green apple,
        and Hummingbird, with one sip of honey.

The next day, Crane set out again flapping his great white wings to the west.

And Hummingbird darted here and there, from flower to flower.

And that evening Crane returned with one more green apple,
     and Hummingbird with one tiny sip of honey.

In this bowl, there were four green apples, and a little honey.

And all of the people, and all of the animals came and looked at the bowl
     and shook their heads, and walked away.

Crane and Hummingbird took the bowl to the fire, and filled it with water.
     It turned into a great pot filled with bubbling green apple stew.

And the people all came back to the fire, and all of the animals, they were so hungry,
     and they all ate green apple stew.

And they thanked the crane and the hummingbird.

Then, the Wise Elder from the Rainbow Cave came into the village.
     And he was also given a bowl of the green apple stew.

Crane and Hummingbird came over,
     and thanked him for feeding the village, and for visiting with them.

And he patted the crane on the head, and said that he would give the crane one wish.

     And the crane, who was a big, mighty bird with beautiful white wings said,
     "Oh wise elder, I have no beautiful song. No one can hear me sing what is in my heart."

The elder smiled, and took his pipe, and lit it, and the smoke swirled around Crane's head.

And when the crane opened his mouth to speak, he had a great voice,
     and a wondrous song could be heard for miles.

The Hummingbird came and thanked the wise elder.

And the elder held out his hand, and Hummingbird sat in it.

And the wise elder said,
     "I will give you one wish. What would you wish for?"

The hummingbird said, "I am so plain, with these dull white feathers.
     I wish that I had the colors of your rainbow."

The elder set the hummingbird down, and lit his pipe again.
And the smoke swirled around the hummingbird, and when as it cleared,
the hummingbird had all of the beautiful colors of the rainbow, shining in its feathers.
To this day, the crane has a song that all can hear for miles.
And the hummingbird still wears the rainbow.

That is the story
        of how the hummingbird gained the beautiful feathers of the rainbow,
        and the crane the great song. It is the story of green apple stew.

You are a storyteller. Are you telling the stories?

Not as much as I hope to in the future.

(Smiling.) It will soon be time.

You have questions you want to ask me.

Questions you may have no answers to.
But we wonder if it is the right time, and the right place,
        to be thinking of moving away from our families.

This is always difficult, and the answer to this lies in your heart.
But you will know more after your journey.

Why do you wish to move?

Hank has always wanted to be back there; I want to be someplace I can breathe easier;
be with him, be among the western people, see the sky.

If you wish to be with My people, we are all over. My people, your people are everywhere.

How do I find them? You already have.

Who are they?

You do not yet understand that we are all one people.
We may speak with many voices, but we are all one people.

You will know.
>   You will move to the mountains, to the deserts,
>   that is your destiny.

That is where your heart leads you.
When you do, tell Hank that it is time for him to write the story of President Redman.

He will know what it is about. *He will?*
Does it have anything to do with the Estancia Valley,
>   *he's thought much of writing about that area.*

He cannot write that, until he has done much study.
>   He has much to learn there.
>   He must walk, walk that valley time and time again.
>   He must look both down and up
>   He must feel the cold wind of winter, and hot sun of summer in this valley of salt.
>   He must sit for days, and feel the presence of those who were once there.
>   This he must do, before he writes of them.

So President Redman is someone different.
Yes.   *Is that Dr. Hibben?*
No.
It will be very important to Hank and to you to visit with this wise elder.
But it will be more important for him.

Would Dr. Hibben understand our visits with you?
No.
So we don't need to spend our limited time with him...
No, while he knows much of many cultures and many peoples,
he does not know much of what you call "spirituality."
He knows Faith.
He is a very, very good man, and he has been on an incredible journey.

But you have more questions...
I don't even know what all the questions are at this point.
I'm wondering about this person we are seeing for help related to health issues,
>   *if this is a waste of time and money,*
>   *or if there will truly be some healing from his knowledge,*
>   *or is he one you were warning us against last time.*

All knowledge is valuable, even False Knowledge.
(As he was about to say more, one of our cats walked across Hank, and abruptly ended the
session with the Old Indian. He rolled over and went to sleep.)

Preparing to Move
September 17, 2002

(From his exhaustion, followed by the position in which he lay down, with the left arm over his eyes, and right hand waving back and forth with the index finger extended, I knew who was trying to come through. So I greeted him with *"Hello, and how are you?"*)

Hello.

I have heard that you have great plans.

That you would live in the shadow of the mountain.
And have the council fire. Is this true?

We hope to. We have found a home in the shadow of Sandia Mountain, with a view of Mt. Taylor.

This is good.
Why do you wish to do this?

For health reasons, and mental health reasons; to be able to breathe better, and for Hank to have the opportunity to write about his hero.

These are the inside reasons (pointing to his chest;)
think (pointing to head) outside (making a circle with his hand, pointing outward.)
What are the outside reasons?

I am not sure I understand what you are looking for.
Could you give me an example?

Health is a personal thing. Look for the reasons beyond yourself.

To do the arid lands research, and also to move into the area of storytelling and bereavement work that doesn't seem to work out here.

Storytelling is good. Is very good.
When do you do this?

Right now it is informally; as I see and hear a situation,
but I understand there are those who do this as a profession.

I do not understand this "profession."
If you are a storyteller, what else can you do, but tell the story?

If you are a seeker, what else can you do, but seek?
If you are a warrior, what else can you do, but defend?

Is this "profession"...
Why do you wish to tell stories?

In some cases, to open doors to communication.
Some people will talk about a story, when they will not talk about what is in their own heart.
But by talking about the story, what is in their heart is revealed.

This is a good answer.
When do you make this move?

We need to sell the house we live in now, first, so that we can afford to make the move and make
the payments on the other house. So we do not know. We are preparing.

This is a wise move. You will have much change in your life.
But, have faith, even in the days that will seem the darkest.
The Great Mystery smiles on you. Do you understand?

I'd like to.

Think on the journey.

Be brave. And pray to the Great Mystery.
You, you must speak to the Great Mystery.
You have always known you are a chosen one.
What of Hank? The one with too many words?

He has been asked to write the story of Dr. Hibben, whom he respected so much.

The wise man, a wise elder.

We missed seeing him by one day, for as we prepared to leave here, he passed into the next life.

(He spoke something in another language.) *In English, please, so I can understand the words.*

What of the council fire?
I am not sure what you are referring to with that.

It is the place where you will call the elders and the wise to share counsel.
When you do this, you will have many friends.
And because you are wise enough to ask the questions, you will learn much.

I think.... think about the wisdom of not knowing.

(Again, something in a different language, then)

I have a story for you to tell.
What story is it, and I thank you for it.
(Couldn't get the sounds out.)
Do you need a drink of water or anything, for I am not able to hear you, but I can see your lips moving.

(Then Hank moved, and a different voice and mannerisms came through; our friend was done.)

Squirrel Stories
January 20, 2003

(Hank was speaking the "other language" and gesturing when I walked past the room where he was sleeping, so I got a tape and recorder. A bit of the other language comes through at the beginning of the tape, and is interspersed frequently in the stories he tells tonight. Would find it very interesting to share this tape with someone familiar with Pueblo languages.

My *sitz em leben* or "setting in life" is one of frustration and anxiety and anger; and this wasn't how I meant to spend my evening, even if I was curious as to how our friend would respond to my life circumstances. The financial ties with the church are going to be severed, in spite of my continued lack of strength; I am no longer considered "disabled" since the combination of increasing trouble with fibromyalgia and difficulty with the diabetes mixed with depression and anxiety aren't on their list of things disabling. I want to be done with the ELCA who has done so little to provide any other support emotionally through all of this; some have actually put barriers in my way. But I don't know how to survive financially without the health insurance they have provided. Which just makes me more angry, scared, and frustrated.)

Hello.
Ha-sha-yah.
It has been awhile.
Yes, it has.

When we last shared a fire, we talked of your totem, and your spirit guide, did we not?
That could be. It was one of our more recent conversations.

Think on this.
Do, do we draw warmth from the fire, or does it draw warmth from us?
What do you think?
It provides the warmth.
But can it do that, without us needing it? (I think he meant "feeding it." after listening to the tape)

It gives the warmth freely, whether we need it or not.
In large fires, it gives out more than anyone needs, to the point of being dangerous.

Ash-chet-ahoya, (...much I can't get.)
I think it is what Hank calls a symbiotic relation.
Because you give the fire fuel, without which it could not make the heat to share with you.
It is interesting that we have learned to live with fire.
It does feel good, doesn't it.

(More I can't transcribe)
Do you know your spirit guide?

If you are referring to the new totem, I would think that it is probably the hawk.
(He laughs) No; Hawk visits.

Hawk is a good sign, a sign that the Great Mystery is watching, and has a message for you.
It is a sign for change, as the seasons change, and our seasons change.
But Hawk is not your spirit guide.

Think!
I guess I just don't know. Would like to at this point; I need all the help I can get.

Who is always with you? Who follows you and greets you, from coast to coast?
Think on this.
Tucker is the one who has been with me the most.
No. A powerful totem, but he's not your spirit guide.
Who outsmarted the rabbit?
The tortoise?

(Louder laughter) NO!
Well, I don't know the story, but the squirrels are who have been greeting me everywhere.

Ah, yes.

I don't know if they outsmarted any rabbit. Oh yes!

One bit me to keep me away from the ELCA, quite symbolic, you know. (Long story made short:
the first time we were asked to speak at women's event of our former church, we rescued a
squirrel that was caught in the commode in the men's room. I got bitten twice, but we did get the
little guy to safety. Then the hassle of reports to be completed, and researching if I needed rabies
shots--thought I was going to die at one point, but just had to get a tetanus shot; all is fine for me,
anyway; hope the squirrel lives long and prospers.)

More so than you know.

Do you remember the last story I told you?
*You were interrupted as you were about to tell me a story, and another voice came through that
was unfamiliar, so I never heard the story. I would like to.*

It was a spring morning, and Rabbit was racing from tree to tree, and to the stream and back.
And Rabbit laughed at Fox and said, "You lowly fox, I can run faster than you."
And the fox said, "Oh, no you can't."
And so the rabbit and the fox went to the bank of the stream, and they raced,
and soon the rabbit was far ahead of the fox.

And the coyote was watching, and Coyote says, "The fox lost because they were running uphill."
And so he went to Rabbit,
 and he said to Rabbit, "You may have beaten the fox, but You Can't Beat Me."
And the Rabbit said, "oh, yes, I can. Come on down to the stream bank."
And Coyote says, "Oh, no, we'll go to the top of the hill, and from there we will run down to the stream bank." And Rabbit says, "OK."

Then they went to the top of the hill, and they ran as fast as they could,
and the rabbit was running in currant leaves, and the coyote was running as fast as his legs would carry him, and he tripped over his own feet, and he literally rolled down to the stream bank where the rabbit was sitting, calmly washing his paws, and cleaning his whiskers.

And he looked at Coyote, and he said, "What took you so long?"

And so it went with each of the animals. Rabbit would dare them to race, and Rabbit won.
Rabbit won when he raced Deer; and Rabbit won when he raced all of the other animals.
And finally, only Squirrel was left.
And the Rabbit came up to Squirrel and said, "I can run faster than you. I can beat you in any race."
Squirrel said, "I don't think so! I think I can beat you!"
And Rabbit said, "I know you have a cache of acorns and pine nuts. I'll bet you my pile of clover that I can beat you in any race. You just tell me how far."
And Squirrel sat up and smiled at Rabbit and said, "OK, when I thump my foot, I'll race you to the top of the pine tree."
Rabbit was very ashamed of all his boasting, and the squirrel lined his nest with the clover,
 and enjoyed the acorns and the pine nuts. Squirrel was smarter.
And that is the story of the rabbit and the squirrel.

Watch the squirrel; there is a lesson there for you.
Do you remember the story of the people of the village who were so unhappy?
Not right away, I don't.

(A phrase in another language I could not understand).

This is in a village of our people, over the mountain.
They were all sad. They had forgotten how to smile. They had forgotten how to laugh.
And they would sit in the doorways, and then would not smile, and they could not laugh.
They would greet each other with frowns.

And finally, the medicine woman came to the kiva, and threw her medicine bag down,
        and climbed down the ladder, and stood by the fire.
"You are all so sad," she said. "You have all lost your smiles.
Go out of the village, each of you, and look for something that will make you smile."

And she climbed back up the ladder.
One after another,
the people of the village climbed the ladder and went to find something to smile about.
One went to the stream, thinking that the water might make her smile.
But it didn't; she was sad that they didn't have more water.

Another went to the cornfield thinking that the sight of the corn growing would make her happy.
Would give her a smile; but, when she saw the corn, she also saw that the weeds were growing,
and she would have to work to get rid of the weeds.

Another went to the mountain, and watched the deer, thinking the deer would make him happy.
But instead he was sad, because he had left his bow and arrows in the village, so he could not
bring meat back.

Another went to the sacred mountain. But on this journey, she could only find turquoise with
veins in it, and she was even more unhappy because she could not find the perfect turquoise,
which would make her happy.

There was a child in the village. And she went to the cottonwood, and she sat and watched the
squirrels chasing each other around the tree, up the tree, down the tree, up the branches, out the
branches, down on to the ground, running here, chasing there, and she began to giggle. And she
laughed out loud. So loud in fact, that all of the other people in the village came to see what she
could possibly be laughing at. And as they sat beside her watching the squirrels, they too began
to smile. And then giggle, and then laugh out loud. That is the gift of the squirrel.

For all the work that they do, they play; they have fun, and when we learn that from them, we
play, and we have fun, too.

We need to put more wood on the fire. It is getting cold again.
(He's shivering-but Hank is almost always too warm, so I try covering him with the blankets.)

Watch the squirrels.
 (more I can't transcribe)
Have you seen my walking stick? I seem to... misplaced it.

(More said that I don't understand, and then he shivered so hard I woke Hank, who said he was
cold from the inside out, and so I crawled in bed to try to warm him, but finally had to turn the
thermostat up. Even then he commented that it had to be colder outside than had been
expected.).

Hot corn bread fresh from the oven. There was a time once when the people didn't have corn. It was when we were always fighting and

Kokopelli's Gifts
March 11, 2003

(I came into Hank's study, and was surprised to see him at his computer typing the line above, as he had only minutes before gone to bed. I walked over and put my hand on his shoulder and asked, "What are you writing?" He responded by jumping, and it was then I saw that he was asleep! He got up and went back to bed, and as soon as I read what he had been writing, I knew our friend was trying to come through. So I grabbed the recorder and unwrapped and installed a cassette tape and followed him, and had my suspicion confirmed when I saw his position on the bed. Left arm, elbow over his eyes, palm of his hand up, and right arm moving around for emphasis to his talk. It wasn't in English until I greeted him, and then he first greeted me in his tongue, and switched to English until after he said goodbye.)

Hello.

Ashayyah

It is a curious way with all people, that, that the sun greets them,
        they think of work, and spend the day tired, one must.....it's nothing.

But at night, they will sit by the fire, and eat the warm bread, and tell good stories.

Along with meal and the stories, many people sing and dance and play their music.
        All people, everywhere, make music, because it is the voice of the heart.
        It is the rhythm of life.

Long, long ago, in a distant cycle of time,
        there was no music.
        There was no corn.
And the people were angry and were always fighting.

And long, long ago in this cycle, there was an O-L-D man,
        and he tired of the fighting, and the disharmony.
And he went up to the mountain, the sacred mountain that you know,
        and he prayed to the Great Mystery for a way to show these people harmony.

And an eagle came out of the sky,
        swooped so low that the old man was knocked over by the wind of the wings,

And the eagle dropped a branch.

131

And when the old man picked it up, he saw that it was hollow, and had holes in it.

And he thought it an interesting stick, perhaps to make a fire with.
And he thought he would take a nap before he went down from the mountain.
He was very disappointed that the Great Mystery had not answered his prayer.

In his sleep, he had a vision,
        a vision that he was to hold the stick to his mouth,
        and blow through it.
        and if he held his fingers on the holes that were in this stick,
                he could make the sound of the wind between the trees,
                and he could make the voice of the birds.
                And even the call of the ones that lived on the lake.

He awoke, and he took the stick, and held it to his mouth.
At first, he made the awkward squawks of the crow
And then he learned that the stick had a voice of its own.
And he sat all evening, playing this stick.

It was becoming dark, and he started a fire, and thought,
        "It is too late to go down from the mountain. I will stay here tonight."
And he prayed to the Great Mystery for something to eat.
And he fell asleep.

And he had a vision again, of a great, tall grass,
        and he awoke, and there was a bag filled with seeds.
He was disappointed again, because he could not eat the seeds, and he was very hungry.

And he thought, "Maybe if I grind the seeds with the stones, I can eat them."
And he did, and then he mixed the meal with some water, and heated it by the fire.
And it was good. And he slept the night with a full belly.

The next morning he started his journey down the mountain.
And the bag of grain he carried on his back.
And all of the way down the mountain, he played his stick, which we call a flute.

It was evening, and the sun was going behind the mountain, when he got to the village.
And the people were fighting.
And he went into the village, playing the flute, and they stopped.

He called them all into a circle around the fire.
He played the flute,

And he showed them the seeds,
    and he showed them his discovery of grinding the seeds with the stone.
    And mixing the meal with water.

They ate, and as he played the flute, they danced.

And the first song was sung, and the people discovered the voice of their heart.

When they slept again that night, the old man had another vision,
    and in this one, he took a stick, and poked a hole in the ground,
    much like the sipapu from which we came into the world.

And in this tiny sipapu, he dropped a seed, and he covered it up,
and the grass grew tall, and it grew pods with many seeds.
And when it was ripe, they ate well, and no one went hungry that winter.

When he awoke in the morning, with the sunrise, he played the flute,
    and called all of the people to the center of the village
    and tried to tell them about his vision.
But they all grumbled that they had no time for this foolishness.
. They had work to do.
They had to make weapons.
They had to hunt,
They had to find stones to build defense against other peoples.
And they left him alone in the center of the village.

Then sadly he thought for the third time that the Great Mystery had failed him,
    and he took his flute, and put the bag of seeds on his back,
    and he played the flute as he walked out of the village.

As he was at the edge of the village, by where the stream made the land green,
    he heard singing behind him,
    then he turned,
    and all the women of the village were following him.

And he found a stick, and he showed them how to make the tiny sipapu, and plant the seed,
    and he gave them each a handful of the grain,

And they each found a stick, and they planted the first field of corn.

This is the origin of the figure we know as Koko-pelli, not unlike your Santa Clause, huh?
Uhm-hm, yes, perhaps, with the bag of gifts on his back.

As the corn grew, the old man tried to get the men to tend the field,
      but only the women would,
      the men were busy, fighting and making weapons and doing their work.
And when the time came for the harvest, he showed the women how to gather the corn,
      and how to grind it, and there was no hunger in the village that winter.

But because nobody was hungry, nobody was fighting.
The men spent their time painting gourds and making pots.

And the old man carved flutes, and they made drums,
      and they made much music, and their hearts were happy.

And that is why today we can enjoy the cornbread and the squash and the beans;

_____Kokopelli gave the people the greatest gift, in truth, he gave them three gifts:

He gave them the gift of corn;
      he gave them the gift of music,
      and with this is the greatest gift, the gift of peace in their heart.

It was then that they could build beautiful villages.
They even shared their corn with the Dineh.

It is good when people share their corn.
It is good when all people make music together.

We need Koko-pelli today.
Yes, we do.

Thank you for listening to my story.
May I have some bread for my journey? *Most certainly.*
You are good in your heart.
Enjoy your journey.

Nistahayah, Nishkahiyah ....

(Hank started shivering uncontrollably again as he rolled over, like he did once before as our
friend left, shaking the whole bed. I caught some of the sound on the tape as I tried to get the
microphone from him and turn the recorder off. Then I kept calling him by name as I crawled
under the covers to try to warm him, and he semi-awoke, and I left him to turn the air
conditioning and the ceiling fan off. He was confused about how he could be so cold, so I told
him the Old Indian had been here, and told him the story, knowing that he wouldn't remember
much of what I told him. A few minutes later, he seemed to awaken more, so again I told him the

Kokopelli story. He complained of a headache, and said he was so exhausted, he had to sleep. I took the tape recorder to transcribe the tape, and went to go fold the clothes from the dryer first, and was surprised to see him back in his study, taking a drink from the bottle of water he had left by the computer. I waved my hand in front of his face; his eyes were open, but he did not blink. When I spoke to him, he said he only needed to get a drink, and he was going right back to class, and he went back to bed. So in case he had more to say, I flipped the cassette and went back to the bedroom with the recorder. He was plenty warm then, he told me, but so tired. Again I told him that the Old Indian had been there, even had been at the computer, and that confused him-- how could I recognize him? I told Hank I would try to explain it in the morning, so will leave a copy of this for him to find first thing in the morning.)

Healing the Healers
September 4, 2003

(Our move to New Mexico has happened since we last heard from our friend, with our arriving here with 4 cats and 2 dogs on the second of June. It has been especially taxing with setting up both the household and the business of book sales, plus planting demonstration gardens that are very highly efficient in use of water. Early in August we were interviewed by a reporter from the Albuquerque Journal, and the brief article grew into a two page feature, complete with color photos, featuring the work we have done with Habitat for Humanity, setting up home gardens for the participants here through our nonprofit organization Hunger Grow Away. In addition, Hank has begun to gather information for the biography of one of his favorite professors. We have also had more social life than in all of our years in Florida combined. So it was no surprise that Hank has been growing exhausted. Just the night before this, while talking with a friend, I had told her of the Storyteller's visits. She asked me to check with him to see if he had any advice for her, too, should he arrive. I suspected it was only a matter of time before our story-teller friend would surface, as he did this night. The tape wasn't ready, but I didn't miss much in my rush to get it recording, other than the usual gesturing and comments in another language, then a very nice "Welcome Home" to this place I have not in my memory ever lived before.)

It is good to have you near the mountains.
Do you not think so? *Yes I do. Thank you for the welcome home.*

I think that Hank is happy here. I have seen him.

How is your old cat?

We worry about him...Are concerned; he moves pretty good tonight; I was just out feeding him.

He was very weak, days ago. I watched Hank pray life into him. *I couldn't quite understand you.*
Hank held the old cat, and prayed life into him.
Uh-huh.
I can't say that I'm surprised help came in that form.(And my mind recalls Hank praying for his mother's pain to leave her, taking the pain upon himself, and her resting during those last days.)

There was once a woman in a small town north of your mountain who was a healer,
some would call her a "curandera" and would bring her crates of chickens and baskets of fruit and food and bread. And others would point their fingers and say "Es un Bruhah" You are a witch!

And she would have tears in her eyes when these people pointed their fingers.
But even for them, she would make the healing teas,
and she learned much from all the peoples, and for some, she would burn a candle, and say the prayer that counts the beads. For others, she would help them to build a sweat lodge, smoke the

136

pipe with them. Then one day, she was visited by a witch, and her strength was gone.

Who does the healer go to, when the healer needs help?

She felt very old, though she was not.
She felt very weak, though her spirit had great strength.
She felt great fear, but her mind told her that she had much courage.

It is often true, that the women who heal, that they give much of themselves.
And don't know how to renew.

In a dream one night, a vision came to her.
Some think that visions are the property of only the People
But, it is a truth that we are really all one people who see the world from many angles,
and all people can have the gift of visions.

In her vision, she could see herself sitting in the sunshine, high up on her mountain.
And she was alone, and she could feel the sun give her strength,
And she could feel the mountain healing her.

It is important for the healers to know healers.
It is important for healers to know their healing places.

She sat alone, but she was not alone.
Because she had with her, the drum which is the heartbeat of life,
        and with it, she can call strength from those that she could not see.

With her also was the flute,
        and all people know that the flute when played
        uses the breath of life to make music.

It is the way we hear the breath of the universe, the breath of the mountain,
        the breath of the Great Mystery.

Remember this,
you will need the flute to get your strength from the Great Mystery, and from your mountain.
You will need the drum to bring you the strength and the healing from all those who are always
around you, even when you think you are alone. Do you understand this?

I think that this is something that I will be learning, that you are pointing me in a direction.
And I think that it is not just for me, but for the friend who called last night, who also seeks your
wisdom, another healer who has given much.

Is this lady, or man? *Lady.*

Invite her to your mountain. Let her play the flute and the drum.
We think of these as music that we make, but in reality, they are the ways that we communicate, the way we talk with the Great Spirit, the Mystery of all. And those who are with us.

Do not be afraid to speak. Do not be afraid of your mountain. There is strength there for you.

Now, have you been telling the stories?
Occasionally; I have been gathering more items to illustrate them. A walking stick that reminded me of you.

I am pleased. Why a walking stick?
In some of your visits, when we have been together, you have needed your walking stick, and so we took one with us up on Hank's mountain, and I found it did make a difference in getting around, on slopes, especially.

The stick--is it made from a tree? *I believe it is; I'm not certain what kind of wood it is.*
When you hold it in your hand, you will feel the message from the earth, and from the tree.
The walking stick is not just to help you walk;
        it helps you to know the way.

I want you to do this.
I want you to ask Hank to write the story of the walking stick.
When you ask him this, he will not know what you mean.
But he will.

All people use a walking stick; the people of all the deserts of the world,
        and all the forests of the world, and all the grasslands.

The stick is not a weapon.
The stick can be carved, can be painted, can be decorated.
The stick becomes a story in itself, it becomes a road map.

You have a new home. And within this home, there will be healing.
From this home, you will heal many.

The curandera of which we spoke, came down from her mountain wiser,
        and not just wiser in the head; wiser, in the heart.
She came down from the mountain stronger.
She came down from her mountain braver.
You will, too.

There's much to learn.
There are many stories to tell.
Know that when you are alone, you are never alone.

Know also that you have powerful totems, and a spirit guide that will show you the way.

I will visit you again soon. *Thank you.* With a story for you to tell.
Soon you will be telling these stories as is one of your gifts from the Great Mystery.
Use it wisely, and enjoy.

Remember to start the telling of every story with the phrase:
    "It is said," or,
    "they have said" or
    "we are told."
To use these words is to invoke the power of the story itself. Remember this.

I will, and thank you.

We have much to share.
Always end your story with a "that is what we were told," and thank those who have listened.

(While I was changing the cassette, he changed languages, then came back to say this:)

Know the places of many people...*the places, or the voices, of many people, excuse me?*

(At this point he rolled over and began to shiver uncontrollably, so much so that the next morning he recalled suddenly becoming very cold. I moved the tape recorder when I covered him and rolled close to him, and then he made an important statement. He usually is done when he changes position, so I was not expecting anything more to be said. But this time he said something that was loud, clear, and valuable. It was so important, that I repeated it to myself, and though I was tired, I was sure I would recall it, so did not get the recorder or paper and pen to help me remember his words. My short term memory has been poor since an illness ten years ago, so while I remember being tired and hearing his words, the file in my mind where they are stored can no longer be opened. That will teach me to make note of them immediately.)

The Roadrunner's Story
December 12, 2003

(We were both exhausted this Friday afternoon, and I fell asleep on the sofa, and can remember Hank out in the study working at the computer. At some point he had gone into the bedroom to take a nap, but then in his sleep moved out to the loveseat in the living room near me. He was starting to make gestures in his sleep, which drew the attention of our two dogs. The fuss they were making near him woke me, and I could see that our friend was attempting to come through, so I quickly got the tape recorder and an extension cord, so was ready. But when I got the dogs calmed down, Hank was sleep-talking as himself, listing all of the things he needed to get done, and then started talking with me, as well. He said, "I am so tired, is the coffee ready yet?" And I encouraged him to get more sleep. Then he was worried about his fever, whether coffee would be good for it or not, then went back to listing all he needed to do, just too much to do. I told him just to rest, and he rambled a bit longer, before our friend came through. It would turn out that our friend had been quite busy that day, as we would discover when we read the next story after this one, one that we found on the computer where Hank had started a project, but the result was quite different than what he had intended. But we also had this following conversation.)

Aishneah, yatahey.

Yatahey, Welcome

It's been a long time...*I'm sorry, I can't hear you [in the living room]; the acoustics are not good..*

I, I visited you, and you were not here? (I think he may have tried to speak through Hank some evening, but that is when I work in the study at the other side of the house, and can no longer hear if Hank is talking, so I had missed an opportunity to connect with him.)
I am here, (and as I said that, I moved closer to him so when his right hand would wave, I could put my arm out for him to feel it. As usual, his left arm was over his eyes, with the palm of that hand facing upwards.)

I think... (sounds like he's having a dry throat, making it hard to talk.)
(More words I can't understand)

So, you have the flute? *Yes, you know that already?*
> (*I had just gotten a Native American cedar flute the night before, and it was still wrapped in bubble wrap, so I hadn't played it yet since we brought it home. It had been interesting to try different instruments and select this one, knowing that it will somehow fit into the process of sharing the stories.*)

I think it is made by the people of the North...*Winnebago, yes.*
It is the land of the big flute people....*Excuse me?*
Different people, in different places have different flutes.

140

The North people have big flutes.
And the South people have flutes made from reeds, and the bones of birds.
You need to practice playing the flute.

But there is a secret to this. When you play the flute well, it is also playing you. Remember this.
> *(And I did understand this a little, for I could feel "in my gut" when I played this
> instrument, that it was different from the others. Though they had fancier carving, it had
> a more mellow tone, and was set in a minor key; I could already vary the tone, not by*
*how I held my mouth, not even the breath control of the diaphragm, although I know that was
technically probably how I had to be doing it. But it felt more like what scriptures called in
Greek, something like "splergidzomy" which translates something like a gut-level feeling, in the
area of the solar plexus, where deep emotions are most frequently first experienced. I hadn't
played the flute since the previous night, but I could still feel the stomach muscles that playing it
had used in a new way. Hank had also noticed that I had a different relationship with this
instrument, than any of the others I tried.)*

Did...Hank has written a story, I see. *He says he's written one third of it, that it has three parts.*
He doesn't know....
> *the one about the walking stick?*
It is a story that comes from the heart...the heart of the walking stick.
You need to read this story......*yes, I do. (And BOTH Hank and I would be surprised when I did,
and had to run and get him to come and read it, too. It had moved me to tears.)*

You need...to TELL this story.

Do you want to hear a fun story? *I would love to!*

The winter fire is the nicest, isn't it. *It is beautiful and warm.*
Have you seen Hank's totem? *Is that the roadrunner?*
> AH! You Know!
Let me tell you a story that is to be told with the flute.
> Will you tell it that way?
> *As soon as I can make a few noises that sound like good music...*
*(*He laughs--it is a good sound for me to hear, as he is often so serious.*)*

It is told of the days when all of the people gathered and spoke in Great Council,
that the birds did not have a spokesman, and all the birds gathered together, and they said, "Who
will speak for us?"

And (in a deep voice) one of the birds said, "Why not the eagle? It is the biggest and the most
powerful of the birds."

And they went together and asked the eagle. "Eagle, would you speak for us?"

And the eagle looked down at them, spread his wings, and said (in a proud, deep voice) "I cannot speak for you. I soar higher than you can."

So the birds gathered together again, and one of the birds said (this part is all told in a loud whisper) "Ah, sister owl, she could speak for us." And so they went deep into the pine woods. And there on a bridge was Sister Owl (said in a way that stretched her name out, like a long howl) and they said, "Sister Owl, you are so wise...would you speak for us at the Great Council?"

And the owl shook her head and said, "I would honored to speak for you, but you see, I am a bird of the night, and I do not know the ways of you, the birds of the day."

So they went away, and met again. And this time, one of the birds said, "Ah, why don't we go talk to Brother Goose, see if Goose will speak for us at the Council?" And they did. And before they even got to the home of Brother Goose, they could hear him honking and squawking, and making all the noises that geese do.

And they said, "Brother Goose, (with less enthusiasm the second time,) Brother Goose, will you speak for us at the council?"

And Brother Goose said "Honk, honk, honk, honk, I would love to speak for you, honk, honk, squawk, squawk," and he kept squawking and honking. And finally, the birds shook their heads, and walked away, knowing that Brother Goose could not speak wise counsel.

They gathered again, and this time, one among them, the cardinal, fluttered up to the top of the tree, and said, "Because I am the most beautiful of birds, I will speak for you at the council."

And all of the other birds gathered and talked among themselves, and one bird said, "I do not think it is wise that we have the prettiest bird among us to speak for us at Council." They all agreed, and Cardinal was told "no."

Then, into the middle of the group of birds, flew the mockingbird,
and the mockingbird sang a beautiful song. And at the end of the song it said, "Because I can sing so beautiful a song, you want me to represent all of you at the Council."

And the birds talked among themselves, and it was agreed, that pretty songs are not the same as wise counsel. The mockingbird was told "no."

Then, into the middle of the circle flew the raven. The raven flapped his wings and said, "Because I can steal the corn, I can feed you all. I deserve to speak for you at Council."

And again the birds gathered together, and it was agreed that they did not want to be represented at Council by a thief. So they told the raven "no" and the raven flew away.

The hawk flew down among them and said, "I am the fastest bird among you. I should be the one to represent you at Council."

And the sparrows and the finches and the songbirds huddled back under the branches of the tree, and said they did not want to be represented by the bird that thought they were dinner, and so the hawk was told "no."

They searched far and wide for the wisest bird, the bird that was not a thief, the bird that did not sing beautiful songs, or wear the most beautiful feathers. They thought of the bird that understood the ways of the other birds, and would walk among them. And they could not find one. And they were sitting there, talking with one another, feeling very sad, that they would not have a representative at Council, when into their midst came a rattlesnake. (*As if on cue, both dogs who had been sitting quietly by, now started barking loudly! It seemed to make him lose track of where he was. And as I transcribed the tape at 2:30 a.m. one morning, the dogs sleeping across the house heard their own barking, and came running, barking just as loud.)You were talking about the rattlesnake? What could happen with a bunch of birds and a rattlesnake?*

The birds all jumped up and down and fluttered and shouted, "Help, help, please save me!"
And into the middle of the birds ran Roadrunner, and he grabbed the rattlesnake by the tail, and slapped his head down on a stone.
And then all the other birds gathered around him and thanked him. And, it was said, that the roadrunner was very intelligent, a good protector. And all the birds gathered together and spoke among themselves, and it was agree that they should ask the roadrunner to represent them.

And they approached the roadrunner and asked him,
and after much thought, the roadrunner said yes, that he would speak for all the bird people.

And it is that way today. This is what we are told by the Bird Clans.

The roadrunner is a good totem. Roadrunner comes to those with much intelligence, and great curiosity, and the roadrunner also tells us to play, to run the race. The roadrunner comes to us to teach us to balance our lives.

Some call the owl the most intelligent bird, but the owl possesses wisdom, not intelligence. The owl knows the truth; the roadrunner knows the questions!

Do you understand? *It's fascinating; I've never thought of it before.*
This story is a good one to tell with the flute.
When I visit you again, I will tell you a story that is to be told with the drum.
> *With this story and the flute, am I to use the flute to make bird songs, or play a little music to give time to think?*

Both. You will know, you will know what you are to do with the flute and the words.

143

Remember it is a great gift, to tell a story, and you have many gifts to give. *Thank you.*

(and he rolled over and started the extreme shivering, as he has done on other occasions. I ran for the electric blanket, which as Hank started to awaken, he clutched to himself, and he knew the Old Indian had been here. And Hank let me take his temperature, which was down to 97 degrees F. He said he felt completely empty and limp and exhausted. When a friend called about this time, she asked if he felt like a bowl of jelly or a limp noodle, and he said that was exactly it, that and empty. I asked if perhaps because two people had been using his body, and now one of them was gone, that he felt the emptiness, and that seemed to make sense to him at that moment. It was evening now, and I went out to read what was on the computer. He thought he had only gotten started on the walking stick story, and that it was about a cottonwood branch. When I read the story that is printed next in this book, it was complete, and Hank has no memory of typing it. I ran to get him to come and read it, and he recognized some of the first part, and then asked if I had changed it, because there were parts he didn't understand or recall. Then, he discovered that it went beyond just the first part, and when he came to one word, he realized this was NOT the story he was writing; it was far, far more. We invite you to read it, knowing that Hank can and will not take credit for how the story unfolds.)

The Walking Stick
December 12, 2003

Part One

The old women was struggling to navigate the trail that leads down to the stream, one of the few that flowed through the desert. It flowed from a cleft in the rocks at the base of the mountain and formed a small pool there. This is where the People came to fill their jars, then carry them back up the steep pathway to the security of their homes.

Once, when she was younger, much younger, she had been chased from the pool by the Wanderers. When they came after her she ran, and ran and ran. It seemed that she had run for hours, long after they had given up the chase she continued to run. Finally, exhausted, she fell, gasping and clambering into the rocks that lined an unfamiliar hillside. She stumbled and fell. Her head struck the rocks as she tumbled into unconsciousness. It wasn't until she awoke that she realized she was lost. She climbed around the rocks, searched under the fig trees and stumbled through the thorn bushes that marked the beginning of the desert, but couldn't find her way home. It was almost dark when she came to a stream that flowed, winding, twisting and meandering through the valley and out into the sand and rock and brush that made the desert so foreboding. It was where the stream ended, forming a small pool in the sand that she saw the solitary tree, ancient of years, all gnarled and twisted. As she approached she saw a dove sitting on the top most branch.

The dove watched her for some time, then as the last rays of the dying sun, blood red and flame orange, fell behind the distant hills, hills that perhaps were home, it flew down to a rock near where she sat, weeping. The dove knew she was lonely, hungry and afraid. Being lost is a special kind of terror, all the demons that hide within the mind appear before your eyes, taunting and haunting. The demon Hunger gripped her stomach, squeezed her abdomen tightly and whispered in her ear the names of all the foods she was without.

"You will starve," the demon shouted as it pinched and twisted her stomach again.

It was when the dove flew to her shoulder that demon Hunger fled. This bird whispered to her, "Eat the fruit of this tree, it will sustain you."

She obeyed and reached through the thicket of branches to the dark purple and black fruit. It was a taste she hadn't known, not unpleasant, but unfamiliar. Her stomach no longer hurt. When she closed her eyes she could see the demon, Hunger, fleeing into the thornbush where it was torn to shreds and was gone forever. She drank some of the water from the pool, then pulled her robe over her and slept, confident in the new found wisdom that the earth would never let her starve.

Then a voice spoke from beside her, "Dump out the water and fill the jar with this fruit."

When she turned she saw a figure that looked like a mountain of butter melting.

It licked its thick lips and spoke again, "After you have filled the jar, dig holes in the ground and bury as many of these fruits as you can, hide more among the rocks and if there is any left on the tree, pick it and throw it into the pool."

"Why should I do this?" she asked. "What if someone else comes by and is hungry?"

"You will control the fruit, you can make them pay dearly if they want to eat," the laugh from this demon called Greed was long and hideous, selfish and cruel.

She started to dump the water from the jar, then remembered how thirsty the People would be if she didn't carry water to them. She sat the jar down and stared at this massive blob of fat, this demon Greed.

"No. I can't do that. If others are hungry they should be able to eat." As she spoke this demon rose up in great anger. It towered over her with a mocking laugh. Then in an instant it burst like a balloon and was gone.

The dove fluttered down to her shoulder and cooed, "It is a great wisdom to know that we are all responsible for each other, and that none should go without food."

Then they both slept through the night.

With the morning sun smiling its warmth on her, she washed in the pool, ate a few more of the fruit and looked for the dove. It was no where to be seen. The demon called Fear stood behind her, digging his icy fingers into her shoulders and pressing her ribs until she screamed. Then, this demon laughed, clutching her ribs tighter, until she fell to the ground. She wanted to scream, but Fear held the cries in her throat until she choked on them. She opened her eyes again when she felt the flutter of wings near her head. Now she saw it. Now she could stare it in the eye. The icy cold figure of Fear was standing by the twisted old trunk of the tree, but as she watched it began melting, turning into water that nourished the tree and the flowers beneath it. She had gained the great wisdom that fear melts away when one stares into the face if it.

"You are not alone," the dove spoke. "Tell me what it is that you fear most." He folded his wings and plucked a twig from the tree.

She thought about his question for many minutes before answering. Finally, she said, "I fear the wanderers, their sticks and the stones they throw. I fear the People fighting and hurting each other. I fear being lost, but most of all I fear being alone."

She began sobbing again as the demon Loneliness rose from the rocks in front of her. He was a demon that wavered and pulsed without taking form, because if it took form, then she would no longer be alone. For a moment it was a mouth, a mouth that moved , but from which no words came, no sound, not even a cry or a scream. For this instant, no breeze whispered through the

146

leaves of the tree, or whistled through the rocks and sand. No ripples danced on the water of the pool. When she looked up there wasn't even a cloud in the sky. She had never been so alone.

It was the flutter of the dove's wings and the soft coo that brought the breezes back to the leaves, the ripples to the water and the clouds to the sky. But it was in that instant that she understood what it meant when this bird had told her that she was never alone. She understood that the very breath of the universe caused the clouds to float, the water to ripple and the leaves to dance.

"This is the way the breath of all life speaks to us," the dove whispered in her ear.

In the distance she could see the demon of loneliness stumbling and falling among the rocks as it ran away from her new wisdom. It was a wavering form that grew smaller and smaller, until it disappeared into a puddle of nothing.

It was as the sun stood highest in the sky and the cloud people were changing their shapes that the dove appeared again. "It is time for you to return to the People," the dove spoke to her.

"But, but, I don't know the way," she was beginning to feel the warmth of tears forming in the corners of her eyes.

"Break a branch from this tree," the dove spoke in a soft coo, too soft for her to hear, but strong enough for her to feel. "From this branch make a walking stick. This will guide your feet so that they will find the way for you."

Then the dove flew to the topmost branch in the ancient tree. From this perch it watched her as she struggled to snap free first one branch, then another, and yet another, and still another. None would break free. She was becoming discouraged. Finally, there was one that was smaller than the others, bent and gnarled, with the bark peeling. This was an ugly branch, but when she placed her fingers around it she could feel it's warmth and the vibrations of life itself. Without any effort from her it snapped free from the tree.

She removed the smaller twigs from this branch, peeled away the loose bark and washed it in the pool of water. As it dried in the sun she crushed several of the ripest fruit between two rocks and rubbed the dark oil over her new walking stick.

That afternoon, after gathering enough fruit to fill her scarf, she started for home. At each turn, each moment of indecision, the walking stick would lean toward the direction it wanted her to go, and she would follow, even when she thought this was the wrong way.

It was late that night when she spotted the campfires high up on the hillside. She knew she was home.

Part Two

Some would say that this is the end of the story, and it could be, but this walking stick had more work to do. Much more work to do.

The walking stick was treasured by this young girl. She kept it with her as she grew to become a beautiful woman. This walking stick was by her side when she married one of the men from the village. He was a wise and gentle man, a man who could settle arguments and answer the questions of the People. They were happy until one day when the Wanderers came up the mountainside and raided the People. Her husband ran out to talk with them. One of the wanderers raised his heavy club and struck at his head. His wife had grabbed her walking stick and ran to his defense. The club struck the walking stick and instantly turned to splinters. The demons called War saw this and they all began running into each other trying to get away from the little walking stick. They were careless in their running and these demons all ran over the cliff and fell onto the rocks far below. When this happened the Wanderers began to shake hands with the People. They brought meat and fruit and everyone gathered around great bonfires and sang songs, danced and played the drums. They took turns telling stories, and, as they came to know each other, they became friends. The Wanderers traded heavy fur blankets for the pots and water jars that the People had made. When they departed it was agreed that they would meet again with the Harvest Moon and tell more stories, sing more songs and share their wealth.

As the fires were reduced to little more than glowing coals, sticks were gathered and added to make more heat and light. The war clubs and other weapons were added to the rekindled flames. One of the sticks gathered was the walking stick. When the owner of this walking stick saw what was done she reached into the flames and rescued it. The stick was saved but her hand was horribly burned.

It was in a dream that she was told to visit again the ancient tree that the walking stick was taken from. There she was to take some of the fruit and grind it into a paste. This she would spread over her hand and in three days she would be healed. It was decided that all of the people would go with her. Everyone, both the People and the Wanderers, wanted to see this tree and taste the fruit of it.

The stick again led the way. The lady and her husband followed. Soon the solitary tree could be seen in the distance. Their pace quickened, until for the last part of the journey they were running. As they arrived at the tree the sun shone through the branches almost blinding them with its brilliance.

There, after all these years was the dove sitting on the topmost branch, just as it had done when she was but a small child. It flew down to greet the People, cooing a welcome.

"Drink the pure water from this pool until there is no more thirst. Eat the fruit until you are satisfied. But, each of you must save the seeds. Lastly, each of you must take a branch from this tree and fashion for yourself a walking stick."

Those gathered, both the People and the Wanderers, were unaccustomed to doing as a bird told them. Still, they were thirsty, and they were hungry.

Some began muttering about saving the seeds, others complained that it was too much work to cut a branch from the old tree and make it into a walking stick. Still most of those who had followed the lady saved the seeds and began selecting branches. They pulled and tugged, cut and chopped, until finally each individual had just the right branch. It had to fit their hand just right, was neither too tall nor too short. Then they sat about peeling the bark, whittling designs, making dyes and stains and soon no two walking sticks looked the same.

As each one of the People and the Wanderers held up their walking stick, they could feel the life within it, the power that came from the tree, the earth, the sky, and beyond.

When they looked back at the poor old tree that had been stripped of all its branches, it was as it had been before. Regrown with the twists and contorted branches that had defined it only hours before. And there on the topmost branch was the dove, now glowing pure white in the evening sun.

"Now you are ready," the dove told them, again speaking so softly that they could only feel what it was saying. "This tree is the TREE OF PEACE. Under its branches all are seekers of peace not makers of war."

"How can it make others peaceful, we often argue and fight among ourselves?" one of the People asked.

"This isn't the tree from which spears, and bows and clubs are made. Look at what you are all holding. It is but a bent and twisted stick, yet it supports you, guides your feet and makes your steps sure and true. On these sticks you have carved images of what is important in your life, you have stained these sticks in every color but blood. It has always been within your heart to be at peace with yourself and your neighbor. These sticks will never let you raise them in anger or fear, hatred or greed."

"But what of all the Others who will steal from us, raid and make war?" One of the Wanderers asked.

"Take the seeds and plant them where ever you go. They will sprout and grow into TREES OF PEACE just like this one. Gather also the twigs that you trimmed from your walking sticks and where ever you find a stream and a rock together plant a twig there. This will grow into a TREE OF PEACE as well. And all who pause to rest in the shade of these trees will eat the fruit and their hearts will be filled with peace and compassion. They will carry the fruit with them and plant the seeds as they go. This is the way peace will happen. When every one of us has one of these trees to sit under, this fruit to eat and walking sticks made from its branches.

Part Three

Now you might think that this is the end of the story, and it could well be, but there is one more chapter to tell. Do you remember the old lady who came down the hillside to get water from the stream? She was the child who made the first walking stick, grown old with the weight of many years carried heavy on her back. Still the walking stick guided her every step as she carried water to the People. The People still lived in the hills, now they tended flocks of sheep and spun wool into tent cloth and garments to sell to the Others who were called Romans.

It came to pass in those cold nights in the hills that a voice was heard, speaking so softly that its message was felt rather than heard with the ears. It was the dove again fluttering from camp to camp, Shepherd to Shepherd, weaver to weaver, winemakers and farmers all who lived in these distant hills. Its message was that on this night PEACE had been born in the village down by the stream. All the People grasped their walking sticks and could feel the power of peace flowing through the twisted and gnarled wood. As was the custom then, all the women selected small gifts to take to this baby of which the dove spoke. Some chose food, warm blankets were the choice of others, skins of wine, pottery, robes, salt, butter, cheese, fruits and vegetables that had been stored for the winter were shared, along with oil for lamps, fuel for a fire to keep warm, even dried herbs for teas and salves were brought by this army of visitors to the baby and his family.

An old lady who had nothing to give navigated the steep slope, paused at the pool of water to quench her thirst and wash the dust from her face. She washed the now scarred and worn walking stick and rubbed it dry and shiny with her clothing. Then, with a resolve that only those who move with the wisdom of the years can know, she continued on, her steps slow but sure, guided by the walking stick.

When she arrived at the place of the child's birth, those gathered around parted to make way for this ancient women, with bent back, gnarled hands and a face so lined with wrinkles that it resembled bark. It was the custom in those days to respect elders and provide every courtesy to them.

She approached the hay rack where the baby was resting. She carefully laid the walking stick across the crib and stepped back. As she did this the baby reached up with one tiny hand and, for a moment, grasped the stick. Then it smiled at the old lady.

She walked on unsteady feet back to the pool and the steep hill side. Without the walking stick that had guided her for so many years her steps were unsure and she became lost. She fell and stumbled against a place where a stream emerged from between two rocks. There someone years ago had planted the twig of one of these trees. It had grown large with a twisted trunk and old branches that spread out in every direction. She fell against the tree and grabbed on to one of the branches. It snapped free in her hand and with it she halted her fall. With the help of this new walking stick she got to her feet. It guided her steps back to the People.

It was said that a young lad, learning the carpenter trade with his father, was never seen with out an old, worn and battered walking stick. It was this stick that led his way to the temples to learn from the priests and teachers there. It was this stick that he used to overturn the tables of the money changers. It was this stick that he used to touch the jars of water and turn them into wine. It was this stick that he used to touch the baskets of bread and fish on the mountain side. It was this walking stick that led his steps in three years of journeying, teaching and healing.

For thousands of years the branches of this tree have been the very symbol of peace.
The walking stick was an olive branch. It was said that where ever there were olive trees growing, no violence could take place. The dove's dream was to plant olive trees all over the earth, then we would have peace. We still need to plant a lot of seeds of peace, we still need to teach everyone to carry an olive branch.

Do you hear the dove whispering again?

"What if each of us wore an olive leaf as a reminder that peace lives within the hearts and minds of each and every one of us."

The Drum Dream

March 21, 2004

(It was late at night and I was down in our study doing some work on the computer, when Hank came and got me. He said he had just had a strange dream, and he thought that it was from the Old Indian. Hank was so exhausted that he asked me to come back to the bedroom with him so he could lie down and tell me about the dream before he forgot it. So when we got there, I turned on the tape recorder, and Hank told the story of the dream in his perfectly normal voice. But the next morning he had no memory of it at all. When I wasn't where the Old Indian expected me to be, he worked through Hank's dream to tell the story I was anticipating. I was sorry not to have heard it all directly from him, but was also relieved that Hank was tired, but did not suffer from the complete exhaustion and chills as he did when the Old Indian spoke through him.

To help you understand some of the references in the dream, Hank had been helping me to photograph the painted cardboard replicas of the art work found inside many of the ancient kivas years ago, when Pottery Mound in the New Mexico desert was an archeological site. We have also seen similar actual murals that were preserved at what is now called Coronado's Monument, but was first the Pueblo village of Kuaua. So we knew these to be holy works of art, not meant for our understanding, most likely never to meant to see the light of day, as they would have been in the underground worship areas. The cardboard replicas are being turned over to a museum, so we were taking the photos for the one who had sheltered them in her home for many years. Hank's dream happened between the photo shoot, and our visit to the Pottery Mound site the very next day.)

The tape recorder is working now? I'll start from the beginning again.

It was a kind of a dream, in almost kind of surreal images, a lot like the figures from the Pottery Mound that you had shot.

But there was this very old man in the village; he walked with a walking stick, and he carried a little drum, and he came to the center of the village or Pueblo or whatever it was, and he sat down by the fire and he started playing the drum very, very softly. And it was a bum, bum, Bum, bum, Bum, bum and it gradually worked into a rhythm, a tune like. And everybody gathered around the fire, and they sat and they talked, and it was strange in my dream, they were...part of the talk was in English, and part of the talk was in something entirely different, and ah, I can't remember now what the conversation was about, but there was this young warrior or whatever, who was very upset that everybody came and obeyed the beat of that drum. It was, he was jealous or he was angry; or something, there was a negative emotion there.

And he gathered some of his friends together, and they decided that what they were going to do if everybody in that village came when that drum was beat, and everybody sat and listened to this

152

old man, then they were going to build an ENORMOUS drum, and then everybody in the world would kneel down or sit down and do what they wanted. And it was like it was just the people, it was the animals too that were going to follow this one fellow and his group. I'm not remembering it very well, I apologize, but it was a dream...*(It sounds like the story the Old Indian promised to tell the next time, he promised it would be a story that would be told with a drum.)*

They searched for a, I don't know, a long time, and they found this enormous cottonwood, which is what you make a drum from.   And they called it the Drum Tree. And they worked and worked and worked to cut this tree down, and cut a section of it, and I mean it was, it was enormous, I could see it. Probably the biggest cottonwood ever, it was a trophy tree. And they built a fire in the middle of it, was how they hollowed it out, they kept burning until they got it hollow. And then they rolled it up, I mean it was just tremendous effort, they rolled it up to the top of this mountain. They had to sew hides together to make the whatever you call it, the top of the drum. And they had to gather all kinds of stuff, again, I am not remembering, they had to gather all kinds of stuff, and while they were gathering this, all the People were becoming very hungry, because they were gathering this stuff themselves and they weren't letting anybody else have it.

Then, its–wait, do you remember the little, almost insect looking creatures that were in the Emergence picture? *Uh-hmm.* Well, this is what they were, and they were tiny, and they gathered-just thousands and thousands of them-around this drum. And they–I can't remember very much, very well, but anyway, they started eating the drum, but they were eating from the inside.

And this group, the day had come for them to call the world together. And let the world know that they were boss. And they all took these enormous big clubs, that were huge, and they're all gathered around the drum, and this thing is enormous, I mean they are all lined up around it, and they began with a chant and they raised their clubs, and they beat once on the hide, and it all crumples to dust.

And in the middle of all of this, are the insect-like creatures which I think were called the First People, but I am not sure; I can't remember exactly. But anyway it's like they spread out all over the place and invited everybody to this big feast, because this group had gathered all the food so that nobody else could eat, and so all the People, it's all the animals and different kinds of people, the people were like all the different characters in the kiva art, only at first it was like they were cartoon figures, taken from, and then they gradually became real people as they came up this mountain. And it's like this group is yelling at them and trying to get them to obey, but it is like they don't exist; nobody is hearing them. But the animals and the people are all sharing the food and passing the food out, making sure that everybody has something. And there is this joyful feast on this mountain, and the old man is the last one to get up the mountain, this very little old man with the walking stick and the drum. And when he gets up there, they have just started a fire, and he sits down by the fire, and he taps on his very small drum, and everybody gathers around, and he explains to them that ever after, this will be known as the Mountain of the Feast.

And something about "whenever everybody gathers around the dinner table" and then that's what this big drum has become, was like a big table. It had collapsed, and so instead of being this enormous thing that they had to stand on things to hit, it was low enough that everybody could sit around it. And I... that's where it ended, I don't know. But it was a very strange dream!

It wasn't a dream, it was a visit.
But I think, (laughing) the funniest part of it, it's like there was real humor, was when everybody is gathering the food and passing it out, and it's like this group is standing there yelling that they're not supposed to do that, they are supposed to obey, supposed to listen to them, and nobody even hears them. And so, I don't know; figure it out...(laughing...)

The last time he visited, he said he would come the next time with a story to be told with the drum, because he had just given me a story to be told with the flute. He said "The next story I bring you is to be told with the drum. UH-HA! And so the little drum that I have out there on the mantle would be perfect for telling the story of the man with the walking stick, and the way the people would gather, and the pride of those who tried to make the giant drum which became a community table instead. I'm glad he gave it to you as a dream, since I wasn't in here for him to talk it through you. But the mixture of English and the other languages, this is happening more and more often when he comes to visit, and then I have to remind him that I only understand English.

I think it is interesting that the people on the kiva walls became actual people, because I think that they depicted some of the kachina dancers and such things, and so some of the kachinas look like dancing cartoon characters, and have very real significance.

And it's funny because the line that comes to mind right now, and I wonder if that isn't a reflection of this, is from the "Farewell Dance" when they ask if you invite your God to the dance, I can't remember exactly how the line goes. But I wonder if there is a Feast Mountain?

I'm wondering if that's what Pottery Mound was, with all of the pottery that was brought there, if they brought it, had a feast, and then offered the pottery in that place, never to be used again? I don't know!

I doubt that they would bring the pottery empty. Well, there's a certain logic in that. It's just the...it's hard to remember a dream. *It is very hard.*

But I think before like I've had chills and so on, and I didn't this time. *That's after you've talked and let him speak through you; that takes a lot of extra energy, perhaps coming just to the dream state is a little easier on you. When he actually uses your body to speak to me, uses your voice, your gestures...*

But I know right now that I am incredibly tired...
Well, you also have your left hand in the same position you do when he is speaking through you,

154

that's it, the right hand gestures, your left hand is palm up, resting against your forehead like that. Like this? Huh.

If you have that exhaustion, he came to you the only way that he could; I know that he has been disappointed that I haven't been in here all the times when he's tried to make contact. With me being at the other end of the house, I don't hear...yah...but I think I will turn the recorder off at this point so you can get some rest. (And Hank went right to sleep.)

(The story came to mean even more to me the following day, when with a group of people from the University of New Mexico, we visited the site known as Pottery Mound. It is a place where people of many nations had gathered to celebrate and worship in at least 17 ancient kivas, bringing offerings to the Great Mystery in their finest pottery. As the pots themselves were part of the offering, they were broken and left there, the spirit that inspired their creation set free. It became the tradition of potters many generations later to gather broken fragments at the site, grind them down and add them to the clay of their new creations, thus passing along the precious spirit of ancient artists and the work they offered to the Great Mystery, the Creator. While many of the treasures of the site now rest in a museum, small bits and pieces of ancient pottery carpet the desert, and those who are schooled in such science were able to identify pieces from nearby, from Arizona, along with artifacts from the Pacific coast and Central America.

The artwork from the kivas has been gone for decades now, but replicas were painted onto cardboard by artists during the years of the dig there, and later became part of the book by Dr. Frank C. Hibben, *Kiva Art of the Anasazi at Pottery Mound*. Four members of the original dig were with us that day, and I shared the story of the drum with two of them, who agreed that it reveals something of the spirit one can sense as they walk on that holy ground. Some group members were hunting for arrowheads, but to me this was a place of peace, not war. So it was interesting that the only arrowheads found were very small, perhaps used for hunting birds. And I long to go back there without a group, to hold the fragments and listen to the wind, the breath of the ancient ancestors.)

Walk Together
in Beauty, Harmony, Wisdom and Peace
October 12, 2005

(It has been a long time since last our friend visited, but tonight I had been printing out the earlier stories and lessons to give to a medicine man coming to visit our home tomorrow. As I caught glimpses of stories I had forgotten, I started reading phrases or pages to Hank. He still has no memory of anything the Old Indian has ever said. But Hank is going through a difficult time, having failed a treadmill stress test, and won't see a cardiologist until next week. It is suspected that he has some sort of blockage of blood vessels or in the heart; he is short of breath, tires easily, and is frequently dizzy. I am thankful Hank finally got to a doctor after years of occasional chest pain, but it is emotional for me, too, to have it confirmed that there is something seriously wrong. The medicine man already has seen Hank in a healing capacity; now he and his wife are coming to visit as an artist with portfolio ready to perhaps illustrate some of Hank's writings, or even these stories. When Hank was suddenly exhausted, I suspected a visit from the Old Indian was imminent, so walked him to bed. It was interesting, as for the first time, several of our cats and dogs gathered around, looking toward the bed, or perhaps they could see or sense the guest. Hank was almost instantly "out" and started the gestures that indicate the Storyteller is present.)

Hello.
Ah, how are you? (His voice is very soft; I hope I can hear what is on the tape tonight.)

I am pretty good, but Hank is very tired.

I know. *How are you?*

I have been picking the plums from the bush that you call sand plum.

I have filled the basket.
Is it not a beautiful basket? *It is indeed.*

It was a gift from the Basket People.
I traded them a cloud for it. *A WHAT for it?*
I traded them a cloud for it. *Cloud.* Yes.

It...I traded them a flame from my fire;
      I traded them water in the gourd.

It... I got this beautiful basket,
      and they got the beauty of the cloud,
      the beauty of the flame,
      and the beauty of life that lives in the water. Do you not think this was a good trade?

It was a very good trade for both of you.

It was the trade of beauty for beauty.

Do you know what beauty is?

It is something that sometimes I could recognize when I see it, but to describe it for you, I am not sure of the words to use.

Beauty is that which brings us a sense of peace, and harmony, and happiness.
Which is the greater beauty? The beauty of the sunshine, sparkling on the water,
      or the beauty of the fish swimming in the water?

How can we say one is more beautiful than another?

There was once two brothers, and they were of the people before,
      and they did not live in the kind of houses that we do; houses built strong,
      houses that will last longer than those who build them.

They were close to the ones who emerged into the sunlight,
      so they built their houses by digging into the earth.
And then, they would take the sticks and bark and bundles of grass and build a shelter over the hole they had dug in the earth, the hole they had dug into the Mother, they sought comfort and safety within the Mother.

These, the scientists call the Pit Dwellers; they are dismissed as being primitive hunters and gatherers. But they were very wise. They knew the songs of the birds. They could speak to the spirit of the trees; and they knew the beauty that was around them.

The two brothers, Nuxswaddle, and Ogwadda, were always fighting with each other, even when they went to hunt, so they were not good hunters. Nuxswaddle would sit at the entrance to their home, and he would take the different colors of sand from the leather bags, the pouches he always had with him, and he would let the sand sift through his fingers, and he would make pictures with the sand. At first he would only make pictures of the birds and the trees and the animals.

Ogwadda, his brother, would come along, and see these paintings in sand, and he would laugh, and he would scatter the sand with his foot. And he would take his pieces of wood, the sticks, and he would carve with stones into these wooden pieces, and he would carve pictures of the mountains, the sky, the clouds, and the rain. And they were of one color.

And Nuxswaddle would take these carvings and feed them to the fire.

Both brothers were artists; both brothers created art, but because they were always arguing and

157

fighting and destroying what each other had created;
if anything, they never thought their art was beautiful.

Then one day, they were arguing by the stream, and Nuxswaddle picked up a stone and hit his brother with it. And his brother fell and began to bleed. The blood was in the sand, and colored it the color of blood. Nuxswaddle felt very bad for what he had done, and he carried his brother back to the house, and he laid him on the bear skin, which was soft and warm. And he carved a beautiful, beautiful stick, one that curved, and then, with his brother's blood, he colored the patterns, and he prayed, and he prayed, and he prayed, using the stick, he prayed.

He prayed until his brother opened his eyes. And Ogwadda changed, and his brother saw it was better, and he went outside, and he painted on the sand, a picture in front of the house, he painted with the different colors of sand, the picture of two brothers, and he surrounded the two brothers with pictures of everything of beauty, everything he could find in his heart. He painted flowers, all the colors of sand; he painted mountains and trees and beautiful clouds, and the beauty of lightening, and the beauty of happiness. It became a rainbow that arched over the two brothers and everything else that was there. And this, he painted this with the sand. Ogwadda watched, and this time, when the painting was finished, he did not destroy his brother's creation.

And his brother talked to him, he prayed, he prayed that through the beauty with their art, they could find happiness, and peace, and harmony. And as he finished his prayer, he looked up at his brother and took his hand, and blended the painting into swirls of color until you could not see the two brothers, the animals, the trees, and the mountains and the flowers and the butterflies, the clouds. He looked up at his brother, and his brother was puzzled and looked sad and said, "Brother, I was not going to destroy the beauty of your creation."

Then Nuxswaddle looked up and smiled and he said, "It is not destroyed; for it lives in mind, the heart of both of us, and that is the greater beauty...that which we know and share and carry with us. Not that which is forever."

Much later, other peoples would carve their paintings into rocks; weave their art into baskets; they would make beautiful pots, and they would make their clothes colorful, and they would plant beautiful flowers in the doors of their homes.

But it was still true that the beauty is not what you can hold in your hand, it is not what you can see with your eyes, nor hear with your ears, or sing with your mouth. The beauty is what you can carry in your heart, and that beauty is only, is only good if you share it.

This story can be a thing of beauty, only when it is shared because, because, when we share beauty, two can walk in harmony, two can walk in beauty; and two can walk in wisdom, and two can walk in peace.

This is the story I have told you; it is about beauty. Tomorrow you will share beauty and many people will be able to walk in harmony, and walk in beauty, and wisdom, and peace.

This is good.

It is in harmony and wisdom and beauty and peace that we both heal and are healed.
And this you would know, for you have great wisdom, and you have a great heart, and you see, you are one of those who can see beyond. You have many gifts; you have good medicine.

Thank you for sharing your beauty. *(My sniffles can be heard, as my emotions are strongly tied to the need for Hank to be OK.)*

Do you have any questions? *I hurt for Hank right now, and the possible blockages in a heart that is so kind. I pray for his healing.(my tears are evident in my voice.)*

It is good that you pray for him. But I know him well, and he has much work to do. But remember even the healer has to be healed. Hank is scared now; he is afraid. You do not need to fear. The Great Mystery walks with you and with Hank. He has a good heart; do not be fearful. He has many praying for him; he has many who stand beside him, many from other places and other times. There are powerful spirits that watch over him, and try to guide his thoughts and his footsteps. Do not be fearful for him; he will be okay. But stand with him, and help him through his fear. Can you do this?

I can try my best to do that.
It is hard when I fear losing him so much, to get past my own fear.

You must be strong; you must have courage.
But I promise you this, now you are not going to lose him. *Thank you.* You both have much work to do. And it will not be easy, but it is important that you walk in beauty, that you walk in harmony, that you walk in wisdom, that you walk in peace, and that you share these gifts.

You have shared your fire with me, as you have shared your gifts with others; we know that you are a kind, gentle, and generous spirit, and this is good. You are good.

I ask you to do this: you must plant the seeds of the sand plum. You must tend them, and share them as gifts, as symbols of beauty and peace. You must share these with friends that you have yet to meet. Can you do this? *Yes, I am sure that Hank will help me find the seeds, so I can plant them, and share them.*

You will need to learn more about this fruit, this sand plum.
It is small, like a cherry, and it dries on the bush, like raisins, as you must learn about the bush, so that when you share the plant you can also share its story. Can you do this? *I will try.*

I must tell you one other thing. And that is to look at yourself as an artist, a creator. You have many talents, and through you many people can be strengthened. You have many gifts to give. You are wiser than Hank; you have a blessed spirit, and you have a stronger spirit; know these things. And know that there is much goodness that surrounds you. You are never alone. *Thank you.*

And watch, watch for a spirit guide for you. Because this too, is a gift of the Great Mystery. The spirit guide will be a teacher for you. Do you understand? *Is it the one who is coming to visit tomorrow?* (Smiling, he answers:) You will know. You will know.

(And as happened many times before, when the storyteller left, Hank shivered terribly and seemed extremely cold. I reassured him it was normal, that the Old Indian had visited and just now left, and the chill would pass soon; Hank said that his back was freezing cold. So I climbed in bed and cuddled up to his back to help warm him, and told him about the visit. Twice he seemed to wake up, and was confused as to why he would feel so cold, and again I told him of the visit, and the chill made sense; he would want to hear about what the Old Indian had to say, and he would instantly forget anything I told him. But I know that in the morning when Hank reads this, it will be of great comfort to him, even if it will always remain a mystery as to how our visitor always knows when we need him most. Hank took his favorite dog and went to gather sand plum seeds before I was even awake.)

(I still am not sure about the spirit guide; what I do know is that while Hank's heart was good, the blood vessels were not; the main artery to his heart was 95% blocked and he had triple bypass surgery. But the comfort that came from the Storyteller allowed me to rest during the surgery; my sister at my side to answer the phone that would bring reports on Hank's progress. And with all the prayers surrounding him, Hank was up and walking all over the hospital floor with the help of a walker the next day, stronger than anyone his nurse had witnessed in the previous eleven years of her work there. For six weeks I was the taxi driver, but then he was back to work, blessed to still be alive. You see, the doctors doing the heart catheterization the day before his surgery had at first only observed two blockages on the x-ray they showed me. But a medicine man relative of a friend had "medicined" Hank, and showed me in the ashes that came from his hands, that there would be three blockages, one much larger than the others. So I asked the doctors to check a fuzzy spot on the x-ray, just to humor me. When they came to talk with me following the surgery, they said it was a miracle that Hank was still alive to get to the hospital, that if the blockage had been any more complete even in the operating room, there would have been nothing they could do to save him. We credit their skill and the guidance of the medicine man with saving Hank's life. Joseph the medicine man didn't usually treat Anglos, but later he told us that he saw the shape of an old Indian standing near us, who motioned to him that while we had brought the relative to be medicined, it would be good to treat Hank as well, and provide me a blessing for strength. What an incredible life we are leading.)

The Children
March 22, 2006

(I was vacuuming the floor in the study, and Hank had gone to bed early, very tired and complaining of a headache. It was a shock when I turned off the vacuum cleaner, and turned around and found Hank sitting in a chair next to my computer, looking somewhat confused. I asked if he was ok, and he rubbed his eyes and said he must have come out here in the middle of a dream. He wondered what I was doing, and I was opening the word processing software on the computer, and he asked why. I told him that as tired as he was, I thought we might be about to receive a visit. I asked if he wanted to go back to bed, but in a soft voice that started as his own but very soon took on the familiar cadence of the Storyteller, he started to talk, and I started to type. At first I could keep up, but he spoke faster and faster as the story went on.

Tomorrow we are speaking at a rural Navajo school, bringing tumbleweed soup and showing the "gopher box" gardens as they call the Abundant Harvest Garden, and telling them about how the garden can fit in the box of an old pickup truck to protect the growing plants from animals. I thought the story was for them, of their history, even if I wondered about some of the plants that were named. But when Hank awoke, I found out that a tree he mentions grows only in Africa or Australia, so the story is of another village entirely, or is it?)

The dream, it was strange.

It was not so long ago

in a village

and among the people there were two children, brother and sister

And when they were very young, Mother and Father would take them out into the fields
      and would have them sit on the stones and the rocks, the pile at the edge of the field,
      and there sits the Great Mystery smiling.
And Mother and Father would teach these small children to plant the seeds,
      the millet and the melons, and the chick peas and the lentils.

And when the planting was done, they would thank the Great Mystery for the crop yet to come.
      And they smiled, and the Great Mystery smiled, and everyone was happy.

And they would all gather the whole community in the center of the village,
      and they would dance the dance of hope.
And the Great Mystery would watch and smile, but they did not see him.

Through the seasons the children went back to the field with Mother and Father
      to tend the crops and to carry water.

And the Great Mystery watched and was pleased.
    And they smiled as the crops grew,
And they would look up and thank the sun for its gifts of warmth and light,
    and the Great Mystery would smile, and they would smile.

As the seasons changed, the children would go out and gather firewood for Mother's cookstove,
    and to give them light at night, and heat to keep the wild animals away,
    and keep them safe from the shadow people.

The Great Mystery would walk with the children as they gathered the sticks and the wood,
    and when they came back to the village,
    they would always leave some with the old ones
    who could no longer gather wood themselves so that they might be warm and safe.
And the old ones smiled, and the children smiled, and the Great Mystery smiled.

Later, Mother taught the young girl how to weave with the loom,
    and how to spin fibers of the plants
    and how to take the colors from the earth and the flowers
    and they would weave the wrappings (here he gestured as if wrapping his shoulders)
And as they did this,
    the Great Mystery would guide their hands so that these clothes were beautiful,
    and mother and daughter would smile, and the Great Mystery would smile at the beauty.

Father would take the son to gather the gifts of the mother earth, the clay, and colors,
    colors of yellow and white and pink and brown
    and Father taught the young son to work with the clay
    and take the pots and make the beautiful designs
    and the Great Mystery would guide their hands
    and father and son would smile with the beauty of what they had done,
    and the Great Mystery would smile with them.

Grandmother, with her cane, would take the children,
    and they would walk far from the village, up the hills and down the valleys,
    and the Great Mystery would walk behind them to be certain they did not stumble,
    and he would guide them to the plants that were good to eat, and were good medicine,
    and he would stop their hand when they reached for the plants that were not good,
    and this is the way the children learned.

And they would gather these and put them in the baskets they carried,
    and as they returned to the village, each carrying food and medicine,
    they smiled, and the village smiled,
    for they would share what they had gathered with those that were ill or lame;
    and the Great Mystery smiled.

Grandfather would take the children to the marsh, and they would gather the reeds,
      and he would teach them how to make the fish baskets, and how to catch the fish,
      and the Great Mystery would guide the fish into their baskets,
      and they would take the fish back to the village,
      and they would give the fish to the elders and women who were soon to have babies
And everyone smiled, and Grandfather and the children smiled, and the Great Mystery smiled.

The aunts would teach the young girl how to use the colors of the earth
      and the colors of the flowers to paint designs on her body,
      and they would paint each other and there was much laughter
      and smiles and smiles and smiles, and the Great Mystery would smile at their delight.

The uncles would come and take the young boy to the place where they scraped the hides
      and turned them to leather and used the stones and their knives and sticks
      and the colors of the earth and the rainbow of flowers to make shoes out of the leather,
      and to make clothes out of the leather,
And they would teach the young boy how to take the stomach of the animal
      and clean it and oil it to hold water.
And they would laugh and smile and take joy in their work
      and the Great Mystery would smile with them.

This was the way of the people in the village not so long ago,
      and the way of many villages, in many places.

And when it was the end of the seasons,
      and days were shorter and the melons were large and ripe
      and the lentil pods were drying on the bushes,
Mother and Father took this young boy and girl back to the fields,
      this time with baskets and pots, and they cut the millet and tied it in bundles;
      they hauled the melons back to the village;
      they filled the pots and baskets full of chick peas and lentils,
      and they were happy, and there was much laughter and many smiles,
      and Great Mystery smiled with them .

All the families in the village did this,
      and mother and daughter and grandmother and the aunts
      worked to grind the seed of the millet into flour,
      and to take the seeds of the eggesi (*what was that?)* pumpkin seeds–and dry it.

And while they prepared a feast
with bread and fruit and melons and the greens of all the plants they grew and gathered,
father and son took the bows and arrows
      and went out into the grassland and the acacia trees to find the antelope,

and the Great Mystery of course went with them, and guided their steps,
and they spotted the antelope in the shade of the acacia tree,
and as the father had taught the son, he went around and startled the antelope
and it ran to the father; he shot it and the Great Mystery guided the arrow to it.
They went to where the antelope had fallen and thanked it,
and the Great Mystery who guided the arrow.

And they took the meat back to the village where the grandfathers and uncles had built fires
and while the bread baked and stews and meat cooked,
they all gathered in the plaza dressed in their finest clothes
and they sang and danced and celebrated with much joy,
to thank the Great Mystery.
And the Great Mystery stood in the shadows of the buildings and watched and watched
as the village celebrated their feast,
and the Great Mystery smiled at how happy the people were.

Then one day the others came with their heavy packs,
and they opened their packs,
and they showed the people of the village
brighter cloth than they had made with the colors of the earth and the rainbow of flowers,

And the people of the village said "We like our cloth,"
but the children touched the colorful cloth of the trader, and then their own garments,
and the traders' cloth was smoother and brighter and they wanted it.

The trader took from another crate a steel pan and struck it on the rocks
and it did not shatter like their pots did,
And the people thought it strange that the pan had no designs,
it told no stories or held no prayers.

But the children saw the remains of the pots that had been dropped
and thought the pans must be better.

The trader took a book from another crate and handed it around,
but they could not understand what it was,
and he called them ignorant.
But the people of the village could read the clouds, the voices of the animals,
the flowers, the fields, the mother earth,
we read the stars at night, the messages of the flames in our fires.

But the children were hurt to be called ignorant,
and they wanted to read, they wanted the books.

The trader brought food from another crate,
  and they tasted it, all the people of the village.
It tasted strange to them and they did not like it, except for the children,
  and they said "This that you call the potato is good.
  This that you call wheat makes better bread than millet,
  this that you call beef has a better taste than the antelope."

The trader smiled, but the children wanted more food,
  and the people of the village were afraid of all these new things.

And the trader took from another crate bottles of liquid,
  and they passed it around, and many took a swallow and spat it out,
  but the children like the sweet drink.

The adults said they had good water;
  another bottle was brought out, the men tasted it,
  and they felt strange inside and they were no longer happy.

The trader smiled,
  the village did not,
  the Great Mystery did not.

Other things were brought forth by the trader,
  glass beads and jewelry, sweets and candy,
and soon the children were not satisfied with the food they had grown,
  or the water, or the gifts of the Mother Earth, or the antelope.

They wanted to learn to read the words of the trader
  rather than the stars and flowers in the field.

And the children no longer wanted to follow
  the mother and father and grandmother and grandfather
  and aunts and uncles to the fields, or walk over hills and into the valleys,
  or go to the marshes to fish.

And soon the children would accompany the traders as they left the village,
  and the village was sad because the children were gone,
  and the Great Mystery was sad because none of the people in the village were happy.

And the children went to the city and they were told that they were savages,
  the darker one's skin, the more savage they were.
And they learned that all of their ways were the ways of ignorance.

And they were shown new foods, new clothes,
      and they were lonely.

And they watched the seasons come and go without feasts
      and no one mentioned the Great Mystery anymore.

And their sadness grew,
      and some became sick from their sadness,

And the little girl and the little boy went to each of the other children and said,
      "Why don't we return to where we were happy?"
      and it was decided that they would do this.

And on the night of a full moon they all gathered and left the city,
      carrying with them heavy bundles of all the things they had,
      books, food, bottles of drinks, clothes, hats, shoes,
      all of these things were tied in their bundles.

And as they walked away from the city and over the hills and through the valleys,
      the bundles became heavier and heavier.

The Great Mystery walked behind them, but did not help to carry the bundles.

Soon they were removing some of the heavier thing from their bundles
      and leaving them on the trail behind.

As the sun bore down on them, the sweet water did not quench their thirst,
      and they saw a stream
      and the boy wished he had one of the antelope stomachs to fill with water.

They left their shoes, their fancy clothes, the candy, and they walked for days
      but the children knew what plants they could eat
      because Grandmother had taught them.

They knew how to make fires and cook the fish they caught,
      the way their uncles had taught them.

They survived.

And when they came back to the village,
      all the relatives were happy and they smiled,
      and the children smiled,
      and the Great Mystery smiled,

and they held a great feast, and they celebrated the return of the children.

Even to this day, in those villages in that far place, they celebrate the return of the children.

It is unfortunate that in the villages all over the earth,
    the children continue to leave,
    and even when some remain,
    they are not really a part of the village.

And they are not happy, and the village is not happy,
    nor is the Great Mystery happy; no one smiles.

No one smiles when the children no longer touch their feet to the earth,
    no longer know how to gather their food from anything but the refrigerator;
    no longer watch the clouds and the birds and the animals,
    but instead watch the screen.

The children no longer run and play,
    they drink the sodas and eat the fat and sweet foods
And no longer know how to fish or hunt or cook or make pots or weave.
    Or take the colors of the earth and the rainbow of the flowers and paint themselves.

They are no longer a part of the earth.
    And they wonder why they are ill,
        they wonder what they long for.

They long for their earth.

(He seemed to awaken and said "My head hurts," and then started to cry, but couldn't understand why. I told him to let the tears flow, for he had told a story of great power and sadness, one of incredible universal truth. The shivers soon followed and he went to bed, then started talking again about how he was so tired he couldn't put one foot in front of the other, that he must just be lost and needed to rest. I asked what he could see around him, and he said there were trees, lots of rocks, and there should be shale, lots of shale, as this was a Pennsylvania deposit. And there should be coal, and certain plants would be found in the area where the coal was located. Then he apologized for resting because he was going to make us late getting back to the concert. I assured him that wasn't a problem, got some of this on cassette, and before long he rolled over and seemed to wake up some and felt cold and exhausted, so I filled him in on the story. I know from experience he won't recall a thing I said. But as he drifted off to sleep he said, "Oh, well, that's what you get for having a crazy husband.")

Cannot's Story: Worrying Too Much
Late Spring of 2006
(did not enter the date and took until July to transcribe this.)

How are you?

It is good to see you again. Ashh...(his voice is strained and very old tonight.)
Come, sit by me, and let us talk.

What have you been doing?

A variety of things..we've been helping your people to start gardening and raising their own vegetables again...
This is good.

And how are you?

I am good, thank you. How is Hank?

He has a very upset stomach tonight; I am not sure how he is.

Take care of him; he needs you.

Do you have any idea what's wrong with him?
If we need to get him to a doctor?

He works too much. *Yes, he does,*
And he doesn't sing, and he doesn't play the drum or the flute, and he doesn't dance.
Tell him to walk.

This is what he needs.
You need to walk with him. It is good to walk where there is the earth.
When you do this,
the strength and the power that is in the earth renews you, and gives you strength.

And you have much work to do.

Come, let us walk together,

What is between the stars and the earth?
Think. What is between the stars and the earth?
Atmosphere, and other planets, other stars, the sun, the moon?

We are between the stars and the earth, too. *Yes, we are.*
Then, does this not make us kin to all the trees around, and to all the animals and all the plants?
The butterfly and the eagle, the grass, and the horse?

Then we will walk, and our feet touch the earth,
which will bring the energy and the peace and the beauty from within the Mother.
The beauty comes when we walk on the earth.

It has been dry.
What will you do when the river flows with dust, instead of water?
This is an important problem. What will you do when the dust fills the air and you can no longer
see the mountains in the day, or the stars at night? *We've had some days like that.*
There will be more; what will you do?
I don't know, because I can't breathe when the days get like that, I have to stay indoors.
You can breathe;
How can we know beauty, when you can't see the mountains; or the sun, or the stars?
Or our neighbors?
These are things you and Hank need to think about, then you will know what to do.
It is important when you continue the work you are doing
and that your friends like the one who calls himself Joseph.
When_____sometime. (By waiting too long, I don't recall at all what this part was
about, and can't understand the words or remember the gestures. I regret the loss.)
Joseph is reading your stories, the ones that you have given to me that I have written down.
Joseph is a man of great wisdom; he is a saint, a power of the earth that is spirit; he has great
wisdom.
Listen to the great sounds of the insects. Touch the plants, feel the life that flows through them.
Think about the water.

Once, there was a young man in the village as the story goes, and his name was Cannot. And he
worried because he could not run fast like the other boys, and if he had need to feed his family,
there wouldn't be any; he couldn't paint the beautiful designs on the pottery, nor could he weave.
Nor could he hunt. It is the custom of most people to lead the young ones to do that which they
are best at, but Cannot was not good at anything, and this worried him.

Another worries, and he went without harmony. An old woman came to him with a bowl of corn
to eat, and she told him to plant this, and he could be a good farmer, but he couldn't plant the
seeds right, and few of the plants grew. And then an elder came to Cannot and said "You do not
hunt well, but I think you can fish." and he took him to the place where the Fish People live, and
to help them to build a basket from the willows. And he waded out into the water to catch the
fish, but the fish were faster, and he caught only a cold.

All these had other ideas of what he could do, and he tried to watch the sheep, but he fell asleep,
and they wandered away. He tried so many things, and failed. He sat, worried that he could do

nothing, and had no skill, no talents, he could create nothing, he could build nothing. He thought that "the only thing left for me to do is leave." So he started walking, and he walked, and he walked and he walked. He walked past one of his cousins who was working in a field, and he stopped and he said, "I am walking because I am worried that I have no talent, no skill, that I can do nothing." And his cousin said, "oh, I don't have time to worry, I only have time to work in the field."

And he walked a little further, and there under the cottonwood, was an old man playing the flute and Cannot stopped. And the old man said, "Where are you going?" And Cannot said, "I am going away, because I can do nothing, I can make no pottery, I can grow no corn, I can not even bake bread, and I worry that I am a burden to my village. So I am leaving."And the old man said, "I don't have time to worry. I am too busy playing my flutes, and watching the clouds."

And he walked further, and there was a hunter, with bow tight, and empty hand. And Cannot walked up and said, "I wish you luck on the hunt." and of course the rabbit ran. And the hunter asked, "Where are you going?" And Cannot said he cannot make anything, cannot hunt the rabbit or the deer; "I can't even hunt the plants that grow on the earth, I get them mixed up, I worry that I am a burden to my village, so I am walking away." And the hunter said, "I don't have time to worry; I've got to find meat for my own family."

And Cannot kept walking the rest of the afternoon, and he was tired and hungry and he stopped and sat on a stone, and he thought, "I worry that I have nothing to eat, I worry that I have brought no fire with me; I worry that there is no stream nearby." And the Voice said to him: "You worry too much." And he said, "I have brought nothing with me, and I can do nothing; I don't know the plants to eat. I can't hunt the animals; I can't tend the crops. I can't heal those that are sick. I can't build, I can't make pottery, I can't bake bread, I can do nothing but worry."

Then the Voice said again, "Then that is your talent." He turned and looked everywhere, but could not find the source of this Voice and he thought as he lay down on the warm earth to sleep, and the Voice talked to him again, spoke words that made him think. The Voice said, "The talent is worrying. Go back to your village and worry for the others. That will be your work." He said, "Who are you, Voice, why can I not see you?" and the answer came, "Look around you, you see me everywhere, I am your Mother, I am the Earth. Go back to your village and collect the worries and fears of everyone there. Make them yours. Worry for others from the time the sun rises in the east, to the time the sun sets in the west."

The next morning he woke and returned to his people. And he met the hunter, and he said, "Hunter, what do you worry about?" and the hunter told him he worried about not finding meat for his family, he worried about it not raining, he worried about the wolves and the rattlesnakes and the bears; and Cannot said, "From this morning on, as the Grandmother Sun watches us, I will do your worrying so that you can hunt and care for your family."

Then he went to each member of the village and he collected all their worries, all their concerns,

170

all of their fears. For each one of these, he would pick up a little pebble, and put it in the pot that he now carried with him. And he would take this pot and he would sit in the plaza and he would think, and ponder, and worry all the worries, and feed all the fears. He would feed the fears with the stones in the pot. And while he did all this, everyone else was free from their worries, and free from their fears, and everyone was happy. And he became the First Psychologist.

You like the joke? *Uh-hm*
Do not fear; do not worry. Take care of yourself, take care of Hank.

And feed the hungry, for this is where you find harmony.

Do you play your flute? *Not often.*
Do you play your drum? *Not often, either*
Do you play your guitar? *No, but have been feeling called back in that direction, and have been getting some music for some important songs.* Oh? This is good.

Songs are important to all people. It is the music, the song, the dance, that brings us harmony. This is Hank's trouble. He does not sing; he does not play music, and he does not dance. Did not some tease him about dancing? *About singing, I don't know about dancing, but about singing, yes, a teacher.* He worries about this, he carries fear.

Tell him to feed his fears to the fire. You are to tell him to keep your eyes on the fire, and watch the flames; there will be messages there for you. There is comfort in the fire. And to dance, there is flame and practice with which the fire surrounds its song. (?an unclear line now; made since when he first spoke it.)

Do you have questions of me?

Is Hank well enough to travel?

Yes. Yes, and he must. He has hard work, that he must see much failure and disappointment. Sing to him, when he journeys.
Will that be listening to music, from someone who is gone, like John Denver?

Listening to somebody else's music nourishes the soul, as much as watching someone else eat, nourishes your body. Within the song is the need to make your own music. It is what nourishes and medicines the spirit. Do not be without music.

When I was so sick, the music went away, and I knew I was starting to get better, when the music started coming back to my soul.

Great wisdom; you are very wise.
It is also important for you to write, to play with words, to create the beauty of images.

171

You must write that which is within you. This is wisdom and beauty, and it needs to be shared. Do you not see yourself as a teacher, as a healer?

If I could set aside all the financial work that bogs me down, I could return to some creativity... No, it is the <u>worry</u> that bogs you down. Go to your mountain. Sit in the breeze; think your thoughts, sing your songs. (And here the cassette tape quit, just as he concluded his advice.)

(We had a real fear when chest pain woke Hank one morning that followed this, and it was powerful enough to get us to the emergency room at the Heart Hospital, where he underwent tests to be certain there were no complications from the triple bypass surgery of last October. Never did find out what caused it, but were given the go-ahead to take our next trip. This was to the Pine Ridge Reservation in South Dakota, to introduce the gardens, and meet some people who taught us more than we influenced them. Traveling with us was Alvin Rafelito, an administrator for the National Indian Council on Aging, who has joined the Hunger Grow Away, Inc. board of directors and is a true friend and colleague, whose quick wit keeps us on our toes.

We worked with a group of youth from California who were there on a cultural immersion, and found ourselves to be the students of two medicine men who will be experimenting with our gardens in that climate.

The additional lessons of the trip there took us from the site of the Wounded Knee Massacre, to the Crazy Horse Monument, and a side trip to the Little Bighorn Battlefield, all in the week leading up to June 25th, the annual day of prayer for peace held at that location. A story told by one of the medicine men at Pine Ridge regarding the history of that battlefield and Custer, gave an explanation to a vision I had there back in 1993, adding humor and understanding to what I had been shown. It was powerful to return to that place, to walk the land with Hank and Alvin who added so much insight to how the events unfolded, and to visit the Memorial now added, dedicated to Peace and Unity, paying tribute to the Indians who lost their lives protecting their families and their way of life. It includes an opening towards the battlefield, so the spirits of the soldiers are free to come and go from the memorial, too. The trip was a tremendous break, and a way to set aside my worries and whatever fears are bothering Hank, and lots of time for photos and exploring the plants at the side of the roads, and watching more wildlife than in the average zoo. And we even got some walking done.)

Storytelling at the National Indian Council on Aging, Tulsa, OK

September 24, 2005 (an email sent to several friends)

"Thank you for bringing the stories home. I am so proud of you." That is how he started his brief talk, brief because he could sense that Hank's strength is low tonight after an allergy attack. "I was so proud of how you told the stories. The ones you selected were good for that group, and they may tell more of their own stories now. Be ready, for part of being a story teller is listening, and now you will be receiving many stories, from both sides....some in the songs that you call poems; and some from this side in the songs people sing, listen carefully to the words; some sad but powerful; some from the deep heart of an individual, and some of the entire universe."

He also told me to encourage Hank in the stories he is writing; that he is a story writer, and I am a story teller, and there is a difference. He said he visits Hank, but Hank cannot hear him, so I offered him my voice to speak to Hank if he would like to try, and he said that might work, we might try that at the right time.

He asked if I knew he was present when I told the stories at the NICOA event, and I said yes, or I wouldn't have had the courage, that I knew he and I would share a good laugh at me suddenly being on stage, and I couldn't let him down when the opportunity came. I asked if he had nudged the woman who asked me to go tell some stories to help out the moderator whose speaker had not shown up, and he explained that since nudging is a physical action, he can only do that with the help of a spirit, one that is embodied, and asked if I felt nudged. Yes, I did, though not physically.

Now, he said, he would like me to read the previous stories he gave, in order, one a day. The first were to heal me, then came those to help me discover myself and my role, and since then were some to be shared and told to others. He has many more I will be given, and others will begin sharing stories, people that I have yet to meet. (a note; long ago he told me to learn the stories of the old nations, and at the event I had the chance to visit with a Tohono Odom woman who invited us to come and see what they are doing to save the plants and seeds that have been around since their ancestors gathered them, so we will be in Arizona sometime, along with a school in Phoenix that wants to set up a gardening program. Also had a fine reception from many others, including Apache and the Navajo friends we had started connecting with already, but now from further west. But several times I was approached by White Earth Indians from MN, one of which gifted us with some very high quality wild rice, and told how it is different from different lakes, and how the harvest has changed in recent years through the folly of white people trying to move the plants from one lake to another, when each lake gave something special to the kind of rice grown in it, which gave each one a different taste and texture; even a little about the ritual used to start the harvest, and how the boats are only allowed on the lake every three days in the old way, but now people go out in air boats and destroy the crop.)

He also stressed getting out to Mt. Taylor, to simply sit and listen for the story that will come to me there. The mountain had its first snow dusting this week, so better get there before roads are closed for the winter.

Highly interesting was that he told me not only was he watching in the room where the stories were told--that session was supposed to be on the Drum, the Heartbeat of Life, and the leader never showed up, and since that drum underlies many stories, it was a good joke. He said I had been called there, to the powwow the night before to listen to the drums, as well as speak to our workshop for Hunger Grow Away.

And he said that he had watched us at the airport; he was one of the people sitting along the wall, playing with this fascinating tool called a computer. Yes, I walked past several people sitting by outlets each time I ran to the bathroom or for a drink of water; we got to the airport hours early to be sure to get through security when many from the conference were all going to be leaving around the same time. Hank hadn't seen anyone sitting by the walls with the computers; we both fell asleep part of the time after an earlier flight had left the gate and it got fairly quiet where we were. So perhaps we were being watched over; I didn't think to ask why the Old Indian had been there, but obviously another embodied spirit had given him the body to watch over us. Makes me think even more so that the Indian dancing with Nora's clan at the Acoma feast day really could have been him--Nora didn't know him, and Hank recognized him from a dream, only said he looked about 20 years younger than in the dream. He looked at us and smiled, and then never danced again, simply disappeared, and no one seemed to know who he was. Interesting.

Tonight he also told me that I had been chosen as a storyteller for two reasons; the first was that I have a kind heart; the other was that I could tell a good joke. So I asked if he had anything to do with Hank's teeth coming loose just before I started talking, so he couldn't say anything--I had asked if anyone in the crowd had false teeth, and of course many do, and then told them Hank forgot his Polygrip so would let me get a chance to talk; they loved it. The Old Indian laughed and said that some jokes are told and some are played, but that was giving away too many secrets. Confirmed for us that some of our strange happenings are not of our own doing, just as we have suspected for years.

As he thanked me again for telling the stories, he clasped my hand; then when he said how proud he was, he raised his fist in the air triumphantly. Then he had to leave for Hank was weak; and indeed Hank shivered for a bit while I tried to tell him about the visit and warm him up, and once he knew about the visit, the chills made sense, and he rolled over and asked me to tell him about it. The strangest thing was the session couldn't be recorded; the adapter to the recorder was on the floor and warm but when I plugged it back in, the recorder still wouldn't tape. I had looked back on last Sunday afternoon with almost disbelief that I got up in front of that crowd of over 300 Indian elders and told two stories; Hank notes that one story several people told him they were glad to hear again, but that the other story was new to all of them, and they appreciated it, too.

On another matter, we have rooms reserved in Anchorage, Alaska for a booth at an Alaskan Native Elders and Youth conference. Quite a distance to go for a two day event, but the woman who invited us said to keep another day at the end because that's the time when all the rural people come to town to sell their art work and buy winter provisions, so it really is a special time to be there. Our friend Alvin will be along, as serving that group of people is part of his job. I can hardly wait. Good night! Love, Tomi

New Totems and Travels
October 7, 2006

(Hank was lying down in the position for a visit, but still semi-awake when I entered our bedroom around 6 p.m. and he said in a confused voice that he was very tired. Looking into his watery eyes I could see that he was almost asleep, and so I told him that I thought the Old Indian was coming to visit and that I needed to get the tape recorder ready. Unlike the last visit that seemed to have been just between us and I jotted down my memories of it later because the recorder refused to work, everything went smoothly when I plugged it in and turned it on, and the visit began. He was very out of breath, more than Hank and I have been, even with me fighting asthma lately. With him so breathless, much of what I heard was clarified by his gestures, so I knew I needed to get this typed quickly so I could recall what some of the words were; even so, there were phrases I missed. There are long, long pauses that can't really be shown between some parts and between some words. Also, fyi, the songs mentioned are all as sung by John Denver.)

Hello. Welcome.
All is well with you?

Yes, it is, and with you?

I understand you are going to fly to the home of the eagles.
Yes, that's a good way to describe Alaska.
It is good that you will fly like the eagle, too.
Do you know the two totems that are closest to you right now?
The cat, the dove?
No, since you have told the stories, there are two totems that have come to you to guide you to more stories. One has been with you for a long time. The other comes to you now.

You sing a song of these two. *Eagles and Horses?* That, not the horses. The one that has visited you many times. *The Hawk!* Yes! You have the feather of a hawk. *Uhm, I think I found it out at Quarai, the holy place.* You have not gone to Mt. Taylor yet. *No.* When you go, take the feather with you; wear the feather in your hair.

The hawk will bring you many stories because the hawk travels between worlds.
You, you have seen the hawk as it brings its messages, but remember,
the hawk can also carry messages FROM you, not only TO you. The hawk carries messages from the Great Mystery; the hawk also carries messages from the smallest child.

(I needed to close the bedroom door so I could hear better as I was having to ask him to repeat himself and it seemed to strain his voice. I didn't indicated it in the dictation from the tape, but it happened often since the TV was on quite loudly in the other room, dogs were barking, etc.)

The eagle brings you the power of vision. You will not understand this yet, but when you are with the People of the Eagle, ask them for their stories; they will tell you. They told you, you have many stories to gain, many stories to share. It is important to know that both the Hawk and the Eagle will speak to you. They will speak to your heart, and you will know it is their messages.

You have been reading the stories that I have been giving you, this is good!
The beauty of a good story is that it also speaks to your heart, not just to your mind, and it will tell you different things at each telling.

It is in telling the story that you understand it.

The Eagle will be very important to you in the next year. Learn much about her.

You need to build a fire, and tell Hank who can't summon the stories because he cannot remember them. He also has been visited by a new totem. It is so strange, a totem will also sometimes make itself so obvious that we are not smart enough to recognize it. Hank has been visited both in his mind and through his eyes, and he doesn't understand the call of his totem. You need to tell Hank that he doesn't understand the song that he sings.
Raven's Song. Yes!

Before he can tell his story, he needs to understand that it is not the evil ones that are the Raven's children, it is all of us. Everyone is the Raven's Child. The Raven brought all the people out of the darkness. It was the Raven that carried the sun in his beak and put it in the sky, so the North People tell us. Hank also needs to understand the Raven is to the North People what the Coyote is to the Desert People... *the Trickster?* Yes! He is the trickster, very good. He is also very benevolent and brings many gifts. The Raven travels from darkness to light.

As the Coyote put the stars in sky for the night, the Raven put the sun there for the day.

The Raven tells a story on himself about how he could not sing, and he could not play the drum, and try as hard as he could, he could not play the flute. And he could not dance, although he tried many times, and all the people laughed at him. And so to escape their laughter, he flew to the top of their lodgepole, and the North People put the raven at the top of the totem pole ever since. He has, he is so much like all the people, that he has laughed about this for many cycles.

There are many stories the North People can tell you about the Raven, but in the song of your storyteller he speaks not of the three children of the Raven, but of the three curses of all the Raven's Children. Listen to the song closely and you will see that your storyteller speaks of the evil that is around us, but he also speaks of the Great Mystery. *Yes, he does.* Your storyteller sings a great song. Thank Hank to write a good story. He needs you because you see with your eyes and your heart; he sees with his eyes and his mind. You are far wiser.

When you go to Mt. Taylor, you must find a spot and sit and wait; while you wait, softly beat the heartbeat of the Mother, and softly play the flute to give voice to the wind. Sit, and wait. Do not speak; only listen to your heart and what the heartbeat and the breath of the wind call to it. You must feel the power of the Great Mystery within you. Do you know what I am saying?

I'll follow your directions, and in doing so, I'll learn what you are saying.

There are two ways we learn. One is by taking into us what is outside; the other is by discovering the gifts that are within us. The gifts that flow from within us, and the East, in their mountains, and in the West, in their mountains, the wisest are the people that always have been called to the mountains.

There is a story told of the sacred mountain that is covered with flowers that in the distance, if you are on top of this mountain of flowers, you can see the dark mountain. The dark mountain is the home of all the demons, that is the home of the giant that the Navajos slayed, it is the home...(here one of our cats laid against his right arm, and I pulled that cat away, but was afraid it had frightened the Storyteller as Hank changed position and acted startled. I tried to explain that the cat had been touching him as it does Hank, and then Hank's voice said, "I don't think I can do this; *I'm sorry the cat interrupted you.* And then he swallowed and said, " I have such a headache" and I reminded him of what he had been saying. *You were talking of the holiest mountain, and from it you could see the dark mountain where the demons lived and the giant the Navajos slayed, that's where he lived.*

In.....(hard to get his breath, but the Storyteller is definitely back, not Hank's voice) it is told that in the place where you live, there were fire mountains and some people like the Hawaiians call the fire mountains "angry gods", but long, long ago, many of cycles of time ago, there was the holy mountain, and it was covered with flowers. And if you were to climb to the top of this mountain and look as far as you could see, you could see the dark mountain. To the north, some of the tribes this dark mountain was called Hell (or Hull??); the Greeks could see the dark mountain from their Mt. Olympus. The Romans could see the fire mountains from the hillsides around Rome. Throughout the oceans, the island people could see the fire mountains and it was the demons that inhabited these mountains.

The ones sent among the people from the dark mountains were fear, and ignorance, and greed, and pride. These were the dark clouds that rose from the fire mountain and traveled to where ever the people were. It is these clouds today that still fall on the people everywhere.

There is a story about how these five demons escaped from the fire mountains. That is the old story; it is told in Pandora's box; it is told in the legend of the great rock among the Polynesians. It is sung in the song about war. But the story that needs to be told, the story that you can tell how these five demons can be defeated, how the five curses are defeated by the five blessings.

Think on this, and we will talk again; now remember, build a fire, and tell the stories. You will find the story you need to take with you to the north country. And I will bring you another before you leave. I am very tired. *Thank you.* Thank you. Remember, use your heart; learn the wisdom that is within and around you, but learn it with your heart. You have much to tell. But remember that for all of us, the journey is one step at a time, one wing beat at a time. Hank is tired, *yes, I know,* I can't, I'm sorry. *I look forward to hearing of the five blessings but you must go, so Hank can rest, but thank you.* Thank you.

(He left, and Hank, looking confused, didn't shiver this time, but awoke and said he didn't know where he had just been. And as I told him what had gone on, he couldn't understand and said he needed to read it tomorrow morning. He did keep repeating that it was hilarious, I got an eagle and hawk, and he got a raven as totems; but he also remembered that while planting the gardens with the elders at To'hajiilee, a Navajo chapter not far from Albuquerque, a group of ravens was always near, and even when he went to get the pieces of the gardens from our storage unit, a raven watched him load the car, so the raven HAS been right in plain sight this week. Hank hasn't written about the song yet, but has an outline formed that will need to be reconsidered in light of the teachings tonight.

Hank said he had been somewhere else and was pulled suddenly away, I suspect when the cat had frightened the Storyteller, but he had gone back there again. I asked if it might have been on a mountain, and he said yes, that was right; and that he saw 4 children playing down by the railroad tracks, and they were orphans, and one by one they would reach an age and just disappear, some to be adopted or taken to serve as apprentices; no one ever really knew, one day they would just be gone. He wanted to write it down before he forgot, but I convinced him to get some rest. I ran out of insulin in my pump then, so he stayed awake long enough to help me get that started again, went out and got his medications, and then went to sleep. It will be interesting as always to get his reactions when tomorrow he reads or listens to the tape of this. And yes, we live on the mesa west of Albuquerque, not all that far "as the raven flies" from several ancient volcanoes. And further west of us is Cabezon peak, said to be the where the head of the giant was buried by the Navajo people after they killed it. It will be interesting to find out if it can be seen from Mt. Taylor.)

(Note after our December 12th trip up Mount Taylor; our friend Alvin was along, and he climbed out of the San Mateo Springs area where we parked, to the top of the ridge where he could see Cabezon peak; he couldn't understand why we laughed when he told us of that view. We aren't sure if the sacred mountain was Mt. Taylor, or the one near Acoma and Laguna Pueblos that is called Flower Mountain. We have delivered gardens to women on a high mesa from which we could see both Mt. Taylor and Cabezon Peak, but I didn't think to look to see Flower Mountain, as well.)

The Navajo Yellow Choice

December 22, 2006

(I almost expected him, since Hank was so tired very early. It had been a hard week, as the time had come to put my almost 20 year old companion cat to sleep, rather than see his health in rapid decline. Tucker is the white cat the Old Indian had talked about as having a special purpose, back when he was explaining totems and spirit guides. And indeed, he had been a constant caring presence since my first call as a pastor, through all the floods and tornadoes, and even was with me when the medication reaction of '93 nearly killed me. At that time he had the spirit of a mountain lion if anyone approached me in my exhaustion, and would get on my lap to be between us and purr to give me strength to fend off the questions that drained my strength. Every sermon I wrote, he was on the chair or couch right behind me, with a paw resting on my shoulder. That matched significantly with something our friend will say tonight.

To give you an idea of the wisdom of this white cat, when I met Hank, the first question my long distance friends asked was "What does Tucker think of him?" and when I said Tucker acted like they had been friends forever, Hank got the stamp of approval. Tucker had a reputation as a terrific judge of character; he had also learned to sit up and beg as a kitten, and he was still asking for treats when I had to gather him in my arms for one last ride. But the weekend before he had a bout of terrible pain; I got Hank up to witness it too, and we prayed it would subside until we could get him to our family vet Monday, and the prayers were honored. Mine was the last face he saw, until we meet again.

Around this same time, we got the news that Dad's cancer had both grown and spread, in spite of the horrible chemotherapy experiences. He has opted to quit chemo. and is now a hospice patient. Perhaps because of the pain we are experiencing, our old friend is ready to present us with an important task of hearing the stories of those families touched by cancer from the uranium mines, and the other pain they have gone through. Tonight I understand the way in which he wants me to be a healer at last. But first I will go comfort my parents and share their pain of letting go. I promised Tucker to free him; and will have to accept that when Dad's time happens, too. As the Old Indian helped us with Hank's mother, now he has spoken words to help me release Dad, which is a terribly hard choice to make.)

Hello. (I have heard the language he's murmuring in, and seen his gestures.)

Ahlow.

How are you?

COLD; but look, look at the moon.

From the top of your mountain, you can look at the moon, the moon is cold and peaceful.

The moon is the little light. But the moon does not give you a choice.

The moon happens. And the sun happens. You cannot choose them.

The seasons happen, and you cannot choose them.

The rain happens, and you cannot choose it,

There are two things, two thoughts.

There is much that happens, and we can accept it, and be in harmony,
          or we can fight it, and waste ourselves.

But there is also much that we choose;

we can choose to sit in the cold and the darkness, and shiver,

or we can build a fire, and be warm,

and we can build a friendship and the spirit of _____.

We can choose to plant and harvest,

We can choose to use, or we can choose to waste.

We can choose to build friendships, we can choose to live in a fence.

We can choose to cower in fear, or we can choose to walk in the sunshine.

All of the history of all peoples is written in these two concepts.

We can choose so much, and we can accept so much.

To accept that which happens, is the first step in living in harmony,
          the first step to being in peace.

It is when we can accept what is, that we free ourselves to make choices.

Look at the moon, its soft glow. It is a cold light.

From the top of your mountain, look to the four directions.

From the top of your mountain, the earth glows in the moonlight.

And that is good.

To the east you can see the good people.

To the north you can see the good people.

To the west you can see the good people.

To the south there are good people.

Tell the story of the Navajo choices.

Tell the story of how the people could make a choice,

for this is a story that goes far, far, beyond one people.

It is a story of all people, in all places.

Do you remember the story?

I don't remember that story at all.

Long ago, the Great Mystery came to the people,

and they were hungry, and the Great Mystery told the people,

"You have a choice. You have a yellow choice. You can plant and grow, and your corn will have yellow pollen, and that will remind you of the friendship of the sun, and you will live in happiness and harmony, and you will know peace. This you grow upon the earth.

Or you can dig into the earth, you can wound and scar the Mother, and take the yellow stones. And if you do this, you will know suffering and pain and ignorance and great sorrow. And your children will pay for many generations yet to come for your ignorance and folly."

This is what you need to go to your mountain again to discover.

You also need to do the following, it is very important.

You–YOU ARE A VOICE (Pointing at me with every word.)

Go to your friends in Acoma and Laguna,

Go to your friends in the hogans,

talk to them, collect their stories, their stories of the mines,

their stories of the pain and the death that followed them out of the mines.

(He uses a breath for each word for emphasis throughout this section, the most emphatic he has ever been.)

I tell you this: if you meet your friends, collect these stories.

Write them down;   hear them,   tell them!!!

Tell them so that the world knows, that the world will join with you to plant the corn,

and leave the Mother Earth in Peace!

It is out of ignorance and greed...

they will listen regarding the sun and the moon

and are drawn to _____ and power!

They (he has to get his breath)

You, you must hear the voices of the elders as they tell their stories,

You are their gift, and they are yours.

In their stories is the wisdom of people

Talk to them. Your friends, friends you haven't even met yet will talk to you.

Your friend Nora, who has known your kindness, knows some of these people.

Talk to her. Hear their stories.

The spirit they are suffering walks the land, looking for a voice.

There is an evil that seeks to use these people again.

You went to your mountain; did you learn that the peace and the power that is within that mountain is threatened? It is the very air we all breathe, the very water we all drink, the very earth that is our source; this is what you must learn the stories of

this is the wisdom from the heart that you must tell the stories of.

You are strong.

When you seek this wisdom, you have within you the power of the earth

When you tell these stories, it is the women of the earth who must join hands and raise their fists and say NO MORE!!!

It is the women who bury their men,

it is the women who bear the children from the glow.

It is the women who can also bear the future in the sunshine.

It is in the women that the wisdom of tomorrow must come.

Do you understand what I said?

Are these children, are things not right with them when the mothers have been exposed to the yellow substance, the uranium?

Look at all the children of the earth, that have drank the water that glows,

and eaten the fruit from the trees growing in the soil that glows,

and breathe the air that glows.

This is the evil!
This is the bad choice.

Remember I told you we have some things happen that we accept in harmony,

and in that acceptance is wisdom,

and the things we make the choices, and if our choices can be wise, based on our wisdom, and the wisdom of the people around us, the wisdom that comes from the sun and our Mother the Earth, the wisdom that is carried in the wind, the wisdom that is seen from the top of the mountain,

Evil choices are made when we don't see, our bad choices, all come from the ignorance that is within us.

Hank writes about fear, with peace

Hank writes about ignorance. *Umhm I agree.*

These are the evils; these are the demons that live within us.

These, these demons of ignorance, and fear, in the end can be stopped.

They can be stopped with wisdom.

They can be stopped with our hands, with our hearts working together.

You must learn the stories of the people.

Some of these stories will be difficult for their owners to tell;

some of them will be difficult for you to hear.

Your stories need your photos, too.

Please understand; inside you is great wisdom; inside you is great strength.

You are, as we have said before, chosen.

Because of what is within you, within your heart, within your mind, within your spirit.

You are not alone; do not ever think you are alone.

Look at the moon from your mountain.

On the night when the moon is bright.

It will show you land that can be the birthplace of peace,

as it was the birthplace of weapons beyond all horror. *Beyond all war? He nodded to go on.*

When you hear the stories, when you speak with these people, you will have in your heart respect and you have within you the ability to know the spirit of others. This is a great medicine.

When you hear the stories of the people, who have lost because of the greed, because of the bad choices, because of the demons of ignorance and fear that walk among us; when they tell you their stories, you become their healer because you give them the power to be a part of the great healing. You are good within you. You are a kind and gentle spirit, and because of this you will feel their pain, you will feel their suffering, you will know their sorrow. But because you have been given this gift, you are also given the strength to take all this misery and roll it up into a ball and this ball you can bury, return it back to the earth, where the source of this misery came.

You will need to learn the ritual and prayers to do this.

Do you understand?

Yes, I have much to learn in this process.

Yes, but you will have great teachers, and you will draw together good spirits.

And when the spring comes, you need to take a gift to your mountain,

> but you need to talk to your mountain alone.

You need to leave the gift of the little lion to your mountain.

The little lion, Tucker (and my tears start to choke my voice.)

A powerful spirit. He will be a part of your mountain. He is not only your gift, he is the gift you will give to your mountain. Do you understand me?

Yes(I barely whisper.) He is back here tonight, the container that holds him. Yes.

In the spring when the flowers bloom, when you do this, you give a powerful gift.

Do your drum, for that is the heartbeat of the mountain;

> it is the heartbeat of the little lion. *He was such a gift to me.*

You were a gift to him. He is a gift to you.

Understand this, his spirit is strong; his spirit will be with you, it will give you strength when you hear the stories. You mourn him, but he is STILL WITH YOU.

He is in here (pointing to my heart) and he will always be looking over your shoulder.

Hear the stories, Tell the stories, this is the gift you both receive and give.

Do you understand?

Yes, and Nora will be helpful, as she has already mentioned how terrible it was as the men died, but they are still dying out there. The miners. This house was the house of a miner; that frightens me. Do not be frightened, for this house was chosen for you because of the spirit that is within it. And it is good. And it will give you strength.

It is very important to talk to the people who are still sick, from the mining.

Think of the gift of the clay from the earth, and how the people would take the clay from the earth and make things of beauty, and then these things, after their use, were returned to the earth. Think of the people, who are from the earth, and each is a thing of beauty, and in time, is returned to the earth. It is the Beauty Way, it is the way of harmony, it is the way of wisdom.

This is the path you are walking.

You will know much beauty.

You will speak of the beauty as a choice.

You will write stories. You will be given poems of beauty and choices.

You are not alone.

And the path, it is a very wide road, wider than the river, wider than your mountain.

Can I ask you a question?

Yes.

How will Hank fit into this? He is very tired and I am worried about him again.

He will help you.

Hank needs to write his stories. (I spoke as I flipped the cassette tape, *he has been driven to write stories even now, some of which have been very powerful.)*

185

Hank suffers from sorrow; Hank does what you call depression. *Yes.*

Tell Hank to write the story of the little girl and the beauty she finds in the mud.

Tell Hank to tell the story of the garden.

Hank needs to understand that his stories are gifts

       not TO him, but THROUGH him.

He also needs to understand that sometimes we all need to step back, step away from the cliff.

And thank the sunshine, thank the earth.

Hank is good. *Yes.* He must help you.

He, he is not given the gift of communion that you have; you see things he can not,

       you know things he does not.

And you two will work with many others. Yours is not the only voice, his is not the only voice,

our friend Alvin's voice will be powerful, too.

Oh, yes, his is a good voice, but think of this,

think of the children of the earth, walking, singing, around the mountain, up the trails, singing, singing songs of peace, singing songs of harmony, singing in many languages, singing to the tunes of the flute, singing to the drum, and singing to the strings of your guitar.

The Great Mystery gives our songs many voices.

The drum is the heartbeat of the earth itself. The flute is the breath of the earth.

But the strings are the threads of music, the strings are the weavings and the songs,

it is these strings that bind us together and make all people a beautiful and a colorful blanket,

of sound and heart and spirit.

Beauty happens. Beauty is our choice to accept.

All beauty is our opening to the mystery of the sun, the earth, the wind, the water...

We were created to know beauty and harmony.

No one stands alone.

No one lives alone.

The song of life is what brings us together.

The song of life is ours to accept or ignore.

The song happens. What we do with it, is our choice.

Hank is very tired. I need to go. *Thank you.*

Hear the stories. You are the healer. Remember. You are not alone.

Give me your hand. (He clenched it tightly, high in the air between us.)

You have many friends on what you call the other side.

The truth is, there is no other side, we're all together. The spirits are with us.

As is the sunshine, as is the wind, we are all a part of this.

And we are all just a part, we don't have to do it all ourselves; we are not alone.

We are each other's strength, we are each other's gift;

> trust your heart.

> (A conclusion in a language I could not understand).

(During the months following this, I made many trips between New Mexico and my parents' home in Florida. Hank and I stayed in contact several times each day by cell phone, and one time he told me that a woman had just told the meeting he was at, the story of the yellow Navajo choices, and it was the same story we had received. The urgency to stop the uranium mining and bomb making here in New Mexico is growing. And more people are developing cancer, especially in the rural areas, so the level of fear is growing at the very personal level. On our way to Mt. Taylor, we made a side trip to visit a special grotto that has become a religious shrine. We tried to go there, anyway–but it is near the mines, and has a stream near the grotto. We had to turn back when we met large equipment blocking the road, diverting the water away from that area to who knows where.

Among the miners was our medicine man friend Joseph, who sent prayers for my father, and advice to eat a little bit of corn meal, not too thick; Dad, being in the South, liked his cornmeal made as grits, but the advice to keep them thin made them one of the few things he could swallow. Another medicine man told us to be sure they were of the holy white corn, as they were the food to strengthen Dad's spirit for the journey ahead. As the next story will tell, Dad felt almost no pain until the very end, in spite of his own cancer struggle. His parting was something of wonder as he told Hank goodbye, and I wrote a poem about the Communion of the Coffee Cup that Dad shared with each of his children and their spouse. Soon I will begin to hear the stories; but my strength was low and I developed shingles after Dad died; will need to learn the rituals of letting go from Joseph or another who knows such things.)

Goodbye to Dad

March 16 2007

Hello.

You are troubled.

It is a difficult time. (My dad was dying; I and all of my siblings had been to tell him goodbye.)

It always is.

I will tell you, something you need to do.
But first, sit, and be comfortable.

When the sun is warm and bright tomorrow,
> go to the river, to the cottonwoods there and take the buds that are just opening,

Taste these; they are sweet.
But they are also the gift. Taste the cottonwood buds, and thank the tree for its gift.
It will give you strength, both in the body, and in here. *In the heart.*
Take some of these buds with you when you go on your journey.
And make for you and your mother a cup of tea.
> It doesn't matter what kind, one that you like,
> And as you steep the tea bag, put several of the cottonwood buds in it.

This will give you the strength and the wisdom to get through the mourning.
Then share the stories with your mother, and she in turn will share the stories of hers.
You both have wisdom and you both need to tell the stories and hear the memories,
> and also share the sorrow and the fear, because this is a time of transition.
And it is important to make the tea of the cottonwood buds for your mother. She will need this.
Do you understand what I am saying?

(In tears:) It would seem a different way of relating to the cottonwood tree we had in our yard. A new tradition.

Cottonwood is one of the sacred trees.

It is a sacred tree in your land, but it is also sacred to the people across two oceans,

 for its wooden form, and it grows all across the north country.

To the Navajo people, North is the direction of age. It is the direction of the elders.

And the cottonwood is the sacred tree of the elders in many cultures.

Then it is the tree that personifies age.

When the First Drum-maker sought the music, the songs, for his people,

he took a log of cottonwood, and put it in the river, and rode it down the river to all the other people, first on this side, then on this side, then there and there on down the river.

And at each place where the log came to shore,

       he would go to the fires of the different people, and he would learn their songs.

 And he would share as he went down the river, the songs he had learned,

       and each of these songs was a story.

And when he finally had gone to the end of the river, and was beside the big water,

       and there were no more people to visit,

he took the log from the water, and cut a piece of the log,

       and hollowed it out, and made the first drum.

And in this drum, he put all the good medicine that he had gained on this journey

       and he fashioned this drum so that he could carry this drum on his back,

       and he retraced his steps from village to village, from people to people.

And then each village, he gave the gift of the music of the drum.

And the friendship that came from the heartbeat, his heartbeat, the drum's heartbeat.

And the beating of the heart of the Earth Mother.

And with each different people visited, he showed them that the heart beats the same,

189

regardless of the songs they sang; regardless of where they lived,

be it mountain or valley or desert, or swamp. The heart beats the same.

He returned home an old man, but he had great wealth,

the wealth was the songs he had collected; the wealth was the wisdom he possessed.

And every place he had stopped was wiser also,

because he shared the wisdom, the songs and the stories.

And everyone else had the drum made of the sacred wood of the sacred tree you call cottonwood.

In other places with other people, the cottonwood is known by other names,

but it is still was their first drum, too,

because within the cottonwood is the heartbeat of Our Mother.

With the people of the distant river that you call the Danube,

when one's journey had ended and transition, as you call it, was time,

they would put him or her in a boat of their cottonwood,

and set the spirit free in the waters of the Danube.

In the rivers of Siberia, the same, a boat was made of your cottonwood,

and it became the sacred boat for the journey to the spirit world.

The cottonwood is a sacred tree.

Tomorrow, in the sunshine, go to the river, and gather the buds of the cottonwood.

This is medicine for you and your mother.

This is a difficult time.

When you reach your family, and feel the pain of loss,

I ask you to envision your father's blanket, and how proudly he will wear it.

When he is with the other spirit elders; when he visits you, and he will,

he will be wearing his beautiful blanket. And this will be a good thing.

Your father is tired, and longs to have his spirit free.

This is the gift of the Great Mystery, that we can set our spirits free.

Remember I told you that there is no "there and here",

there is "all together;" that is the gift of the Great Mystery, as well.

You will be given signs that your father's spirit is with you.

And know that your father will now be free to make the jokes

      and share the humor that he has felt restrained,

and he will be free to share his stories with you, share the wisdom,

      with you in the way that the spirits communicate with us, when we are still of the flesh.

Do you know what I am saying?

I am not sure how the spirits communicate with us.

You will know. And it will be good.

Is it in the dream time?

Often.

But understand, for those who gained entry to the spirit world,

      distance means nothing,

      time means nothing,

      Love is universal and means everything.

Love is the energy of the spirit.

The answer to that is the energy of the spirit, we do not need to fear,

      it is the transition for the spirits themselves. *(A confusing line from the tape.)*

Do you have any questions?

Yes, is there any message for my sister who respects you so much?
And is leaving his side early tomorrow morning to go back to Arizona?

Tell her the same thing I have told you.
What I have told you is for all people everywhere,
but for you and your family at this time, you all need to let yourselves grieve the loss
but you also need to rejoice in what the spirit has gained.

And one of the things that is important that each of you needs to envision the blanket your father
will wear, the blanket he wove with so much kindness, so much generosity, so much goodness.

His is a truly beautiful blanket.

And he will finish it soon.

All but one thread....*Excuse me?*
The blanket is finished, will be finished, all but one thread,
and that is the thread that connects him to you and each member of the family.

We all finish our blankets except for one thread.

The flowers are beautiful, and among some people, there is a saying,
        "It is a good day to die."
Your father will know when it is a good day to die.

And for you, and your mother, and your family, it will be a sad day,
        but your father will be rejoicing as he is greeted by old friends, old family,
        and his dogs will greet him and walk with him on the pathway,
        as he wraps himself in the blanket,
        he will possess more wisdom than he knew existed;
and will look back at us, and he will laugh at how shallow we all are,
        how limited our understanding is.

(From scripture) *"For now we see through the mirror darkly, but then shall see face to face.."*

These are not the words of any single group.

>These are of all people.

And we are each one of us, the flowers in the Great Mystery's garden.

>That's why the sun shines on us every day.

It is important that you rest, because your family will need your strength,

>they will need your understanding,

>they will need your wisdom,

>they will need your heart.

Will I be there with my mother when Dad's transition is made, or will it happen before I arrive?

I think you will be there; *I know you don't know for sure. (I arrived a day late, which would have been Dad's birthday.)*

But when the transition occurs, the space, the distance, the time, means nothing anymore.

And this is good.

 Just as with the sadness,

I knew he was struggling tonight, it didn't matter how far apart we were.

You knew this, you know this in your heart. *Yes.*

Do not be afraid to weep. It is how we express, it is the strength of feeling, it is the gift of love.

Time and distance and what else will not make the difference when he makes the transition?

Time, and space, and distance, *Space and distance are different?*

Space is place, *distance is what is between places.* Yes.

When the north wind wraps its arms around your father,

>as he pulls his blanket around him, in peace he steps,

you will also feel some of his relief and his joy, and this will confuse you,

>because you will also be feeling pain and loss and grief, and these are normal and natural

>but you will also feel your father's sense of wonder and joy.

As I did with my friend Scott, when the cloud of sadness lifted, I knew; the music I was looking at went from sorrow to joyful hymns, because he was where he longed to be, and his suffering was all over.

So I am not unprepared to feel that with Dad.

Remember the cottonwood; remember the story

of the Danube, and in Siberia?

The story of the seeker of the songs, the maker of the drum.

Who went down the river and came back and shared the wisdom.

Think on that story.

And pray to the Great Mystery a prayer of thanks for your father.

Pray for thanks in the wisdom he will be gaining.

Pray in thanks for the pain he did not know.

And pray thanks for the time you had to spend with him.

For these are gifts.

Drink the tea; it is good.

For one who has had thoughts, it will help anticipate your loss.

It is good? Yes.

Remember it is important, to let your heart weep.(*And when I drank the tea, the tears flowed.*)

Hank is very tired, and I must go now. *Thank you. Dawai.*

Ah, you speak of the Pueblo people.

Please look after Hank while I travel.

Hank has much to do; know that we are always with him, as we are always with you.

Thank you, and thank you for honoring him by letting him rest,

but for coming to help me prepare for what this next week, month or days will bring.

Know that your mother will need your strength and your wisdom and your love.

In Conclusion....

And so, dear reader, we entrust these visits and lessons to your care.

For they are not OUR stories at all;
they are the stories of all peoples.

We receive them in a most unusual way,
frequently in times of crises or great need.

May the power of the stories
instruct us, inspire us, and motivate us
to enjoy diversity,
to celebrate the gifts of all creation,
to seek a profound peace within each soul,
and to weave voices together in harmony.

And most of all, may we seek to honor the Great Mystery
in everything we do, giving thanks for each new day.

About Tomi Jill Folk and Hank Bruce

It wasn't love at first sight, but love at first read,
and the plants and pets they adored, that brought them together.

Tomi grew up with her parents, one sister and two brothers in the small town of Hunter, ND. She was safe to ride her bike anywhere for her Sunday morning paper route where she was technically a Newspaper Boy, as there were no paper carriers or delivery people just yet. It was easy to go see her grandparents before or after school, since they lived near by. She started working as a babysitter at an early age, then was offered jobs on a truck farm, and in the local grocery store, where she knew most of the customers by name. She still found time to be involved in many school activities, and attended North Dakota State University in Fargo, ND, and then graduated from Concordia College, Moorhead, MN. But the love of her life during that time was her work at Red Willow Bible Camp, serving youth from churches throughout the eastern half of the state of North Dakota. She attended and graduated from Luther Northwestern Seminary in St. Paul, MN. Over her years of congregational ministry, she served churches in ND, MT, AZ, MN, SD, and FL.

During that time, her churches went through three national disasters due to flooding, and one also had a tornado impact nearby. Physical exhaustion was complicated by a medication reaction that nearly killed her, and was the reason she moved to Florida to recover near her parents, who had retired there.

*****

Hank grew up on a farm near Aliquippa, PA and it is said he could name every plant in the garden and woods by the time that he could walk. He and his parents and two brothers were also hard workers, with Hank's life complicated by severe asthma. He found relief and strength when he attended the University of New Mexico in Albuquerque. He married while teaching and writing horticulture articles back in Pennsylvania, and became the father of one daughter. The three moved to Florida, where various jobs paid the bills while he continued his passion with the pen. Hank currently has twenty books published, and was recently awarded the Florida chapter of the American Horticultural Therapy Association's Lifetime Achievement Award.

Hank was managing a store and teaching writing classes when Tomi arrived in Florida. She had been compelled to write poetry while recovering, but needed an objective reader to determine if any of it was of value. Hank was newly divorced and a new grandfather when Tomi took one of his classes. He read her poetry, she read his writing, both the humorous gardening books and his fiction: short stories and several novels. She tricked him into proposing on the second date, and he tricked her into saying yes. They married within months, and the roller coaster of activity has never slowed since.

*****

Today Tomi and Hank keep busy from their home in a suburb of Albuquerque. Petals & Pages Press gives them a means to sell their writing, such as *Global Gardening.* They travel as public speakers on the topics of horticultural therapy, and fighting hunger with family and community gardens, using storytelling and humor to deliver their serious messages. They are co-founders and officers of the nonprofit Hunger Grow Away, Inc. which partners with groups and individuals to have micro-intensive gardens growing multi-purpose, continuous harvest plants around the world. They encourage you to check the organization's website at www.hungergrowaway.com . They enjoy their three grandchildren in FL, and pets at home.

www.ingramcontent.com/pod-product-compliance
Lightning Source LLC
Chambersburg PA
CBHW080821020726

47501CB00009B/2369